PENGUIN BOOKS
# HEDON

Priyanka Mookerjee is engaged in what appears to be a lifelong battle to understand modern technology. She has learnt how to use a computer and google things, but the finer points of smartphones and Wi-Fi still elude her. She copes with all the stress by reading, eating too much cake and writing. This is her first novel.

# HEDON

## Priyanka

PENGUIN BOOKS

An imprint of Penguin Random House

PENGUIN BOOKS

USA | Canada | UK | Ireland | Australia
New Zealand | India | South Africa | China | Singapore

Penguin Books is part of the Penguin Random House group of companies
whose addresses can be found at global.penguinrandomhouse.com

Published by Penguin Random House India Pvt. Ltd
4th Floor, Capital Tower 1, MG Road,
Gurugram 122 002, Haryana, India

Penguin
Random House
India

First published by Penguin Books India 2016

Copyright © Priyanka Mookerjee 2016

All rights reserved

10 9 8 7 6 5 4 3 2

This is a work of fiction. Names, characters, places and incidents are either the
product of the author's imagination or are used fictitiously, and any resemblance
to any actual person, living or dead, events or locales is entirely coincidental.

ISBN 9780143425953

Typeset in Adobe Caslon Pro by R. Ajith Kumar, New Delhi

Printed at Repro India Limited

This book is sold subject to the condition that it shall not, by way of trade
or otherwise, be lent, resold, hired out, or otherwise circulated without the
publisher's prior consent in any form of binding or cover other than that in
which it is published and without a similar condition including this condition
being imposed on the subsequent purchaser.

www.penguin.co.in

This is a legitimate digitally printed version of the book and therefore might not
have certain extra finishing on the cover.

*For my grandfather, who told me to learn the rules
before breaking them*

# Button & the Small Fry

*Tars, can you please stop grinning at the blackboard? Basu's going to think we're up to something.*

Yeah and it's creeping me out.

I read the note dropped on to my desk and gave Button and Cookie a discreet finger, holding up the glossy cover of *Macbeth* as a shield.

My ponytail took a dive backwards, taking my head with it, and I yelped loudly.

'Nayantara and Atreyi, please leave the room.' Rina Basu, our stolid English teacher, dismissed us without any fuss, returning unruffled to her discourse on the complex conflation of the male and female within Lady Macbeth and the three witches.

It was interesting stuff, sure, but I had more important things to discuss.

Cookie shot us a reproachful glare as we exited the classroom, shaking with the effort of holding in our laughter and glee till we were safely outside. The first day back in school after the winter holidays, and we had already got ourselves kicked out

1

of class. Cookie didn't approve at all, but really, we had been perfectly sensible about it and chosen the least hysterical teacher to piss off, even if it was the *only* class that was actually tolerable to sit through.

'Okay, so.' Button turned to me as we walked down the corridor, heading towards our favourite library. 'What was all that grinning about?'

I told her. She held her stride and shook her head.

'Why didn't you call me right after it happened? Moron.'

'I did! Thrice! Your mom told me you were studying each time.'

Button sighed. 'She's gone nuts with these stupid board exams coming up.'

'She hates me, I think.'

'She hates all my distractions. Whatever. Tell me what the deal is, then? You met this guy—'

'Man.'

'Okay fine, you met this *man*—'

'Actually, gentleman—'

'I'll kill you.'

I sniggered. 'All right, all right. Go on—'

'So you meet him at the wedding, you talk, you dance, and then what? What about the other parties? Did you see him again?'

I hadn't. Not for lack of trying, of course. I had acquired the habit of scanning every room I entered, alternating between apprehension and hope. It was to no avail, however. The liveried kept trailing champagne around cocktail hours and dinners and receptions until, finally, the suspended week celebrating the wedding drew to a close. I had averted my eyes from the carcasses of the last party as we drove away from the fort, taking the executive decision to not spoil a happy illusion with images of dark, wiry men pulling down colourful canopies and dead fairy lights, exposing the splintery beams beneath.

'Nope. Didn't spot him anywhere. He must've left.'

'So, what? That's it? You're just never going to meet him again? And that's that?'

'Well, he gave me his card and told me to call or email him if I ever needed help, or just to talk.'

'What did you say?'

'I think I said I would, but I don't really remember.'

'*La-ame*. Give me more details. Where's he from? What does he do?'

'Delhi. Don't know what he does, but the name on his card is Vijay Dhillon.'

'Woah, wait. Is he one of *the* Dhillons? Dhillon Paints and Fans and whatnot?'

'I think so. Simi didn't know jack. All she said was that he's a friend of her sister's and had just graduated from Princeton. Her mum's been bugging her to ask him to help with her college essays.'

'That's it, then! That's what you should do!'

'What? Bug Simi? You know she doesn't even want to go to college—'

'God, you're dumb. Ask him for help with your essays!'

'I don't need help with my college essays.'

'You haven't even started on one yet! I heard that Zarine bitch bragging about how she's already done with all of hers.'

'Seriously? Fuck. Fine, I'll ask for help. He'll probably be good, too. Seemed like he was super smart. Quoted this philosopher person and everything.'

As we approached the library, Button stopped short. 'Dammit. I hope Basu doesn't go off nipping to Roshan after class.'

'Shit. Yeah.' It was an unwritten pact between us that however much we pissed off every other staff member, we would never bother our vice principal, Dr Roshan. Mrs Basu was quite a good sort, but rules were rules, and The House had nothing in as much abundance as it did rules.

We looked at each other, concentrating. Button bit her lip and I scrunched up my eyes, both of us following the path of our conjoined thoughts without words. For a second, I dwelled on how infinitely better my life was with her in it, and I think now that sometimes we recognize moments of true happiness only after they've passed us by.

I came to a conclusion. 'So, we have to get Roshan out of the office in the break between periods. Basu won't bother complaining if she can't find her right away, I don't think.'

'But how?'

'Say that she's needed somewhere for something?'

'Too risky. We'll wind up with two ends to cover.' Button was a firm believer in minimizing risk.

'So we make sure that whatever reason we give her to leave the office is a solid one.'

'Well, I could go pretend to have a fall while walking past her room. You know how she is—she'll insist on taking me to the nurse herself if I yowl loud enough.'

I nodded consensus. 'Yeah, that'll work. But let's get one of the minions to do it? I still have more obsessing to do.'

'Bloody minions can't do anything right, man. Remember when we used that idiot chit from class five to tell The Raccoon they'd seen a mouse in Wood Hall? Stupid goat made a complete hack job of it. We didn't even get twenty free minutes in the period!'

'We'll pick something easy then . . . fainting! She can pretend to faint. No talking required.'

'Fine. Let's go over to the junior side now and find one.'

'Button?'

'Tars?'

'We are terrible people.'

We looked at each other, again. We willed ourselves not to laugh, again. And then we laughed a little, and then we laughed a lot, because yes, yes we were terrible people, but we were also young and brilliant and irreverent, and our lives gleamed heady and victorious ahead of us.

I noticed a little girl, probably from the third or fourth grade, trotting down one of the innumerable winding dark staircases that dotted The House.

Built for India's governor general during the late nineteenth century, the grand Gothic towers of The House still imbue Calcutta's skyline with a claim to architectural pride. All us girls who spent over a decade of our lives walking in through the arching green gates of The House carry the school around with us for the rest of our days, in the ankles we can never uncross, the backs we can never slouch, in the pleases and thankyous and old-fashioned curtsies that are now ingrained in us. In the sense of being set apart, of belonging to a privileged club removed in both space and time from the loud, sweaty, dirty city outside.

Inside, bookshelves are lined with *William* and Wodehouse, staffrooms are lined with Dickensian relics, and classrooms spend more time dispensing etiquette than economics.

'Oi, small fry! C'mere.'

In the years before the Internet grew kids up before it was time to grow up, the pecking order of seniority still held great rank in school. Unwavering obedience, cited as honourable loyalty, was insisted upon, the looming threat of ostracization maintaining our order for us.

And so, the tiny junior clutched her fat red water bottle to her chest and blinked apprehensively at us, her eyes wide and not just a little afraid.

'Listen up. You need to go and pretend to faint outside Dr Roshan's office. Give us away and you're dead, understand?'

The small fry looked terrified enough at the idea to give us hope that she might not even have to fake the faint.

———

Having sent Small Fry off to take care of business, we settled into the woven cane chairs in a secluded nook at the back of the library. Our black Mary Janes dangled above cold grey stone, and Button listened with tempered excitement, cocking an eyebrow in trepidation as her friend, who generally suffered from verbal tirades and tangents, struggled to answer the basic, scary, inexplicable question—why?

I shook my head, trying to find the words. 'It was so weird, Button. Like all these random thoughts and memories rushed into my—not even head, no. Like, into my senses or something. The colour of sunlight at three in the afternoon and the smell of unplucked lavender and an image of the house I was born in but don't even remember. I guess it felt, I don't know, inevitable?'

I broke off at Button's expression, somewhere between mirth and nausea. 'Shut up!'

'I didn't say anything!'

'Shut UP!'

'Call him tonight.'

'I'll slap your ugly face.'

'He gave you his number! Just send him a message!'

'No.'

'Say that again.'

'No—ow! Don't punch me!'

'Send him a message, then.'

'FINE!'

She snorted, satisfied. 'How old is he?'

'No idea. Old.' I thought about the information at hand, tried to do the math. 'Maybe twenty-four or something.'

'Holy shit! That's almost twenty-five!'

'He's a hot fossil.'

'A dashing dinosaur.'

'A regal relic!'

'Sexy uncleji?'

'Too much. Listen, read this. Wrote it when I got home yesterday.'

'Instead of doing the psych project. Idiot.'

'Whatever, I'm topping the class anyway.'

'Zarine's catching up, though. She got two marks more than you on the last test.'

'Shut up and read it.'

Button finished reading the crinkled page torn out from my favourite notebook and nodded. Looking very serious—a rare look on her—she gathered up my holes and buttoned them into place.

'It's really nice, Tars. But let's not tell anyone except Cookie about this.'

'Wasn't planning on it, but why?'

She folded up the sheet and slipped it into her pocket. 'Because *we* don't care that you're a raving loon.'

———

Button was, as always, just convincing me that it was okay to want what I wanted. She couldn't have known then how it would go on to change the very fabric of the air around me, flush as it was thereafter, with a million tingling frequencies.

You see, when Jay Dhillon walked into my life, I was labouring under that omnipresent delusion of youth, convinced the world was mine for the taking.

With the discovery of purpose, I realized the loss of my freedom. But this was before that bothered me. It was before I learned that nothing is ever what it seems, and that our lies are just dressed up versions of hopeful truths—they are dreams.

Besides, it was one of those things that happened because it had to. The universe had built me in such a way that had Jay and I met inside fading bodies, closer to ash than flesh, at eighty-three, I could not have but lost myself to him just as instantly, just as irrevocably. And I suppose that is what made the whole matter so terribly sad. The inevitability of it, you know; discarded time and irrelevant space.

This was always going to happen.

# Caroline's Ship

It was a grand party, unfolding, as all grand parties do, in a full swing of champagne, ribbons, livery and politics.

Devika Das was getting married. But that means nothing, of course. It was Debi Mullick's eldest granddaughter getting married.

Debi Mullick had been Chief Minister of West Bengal for thirty-four years now. In that time, he had established an authoritarian rule, while cloaked in the genteel figure of a soft-spoken barrister. The state had slowly crumbled; dust from what remained of business and industry mingled with the ashes of bureaucracy, even as people took to the streets waving loyal red flags. And through it all, Debi Mullick had sat upon a simple throne, gilded only ever so slightly, a sombre expression upon his pleasant face.

I was there because Devika's younger sister, Simi, and I had been close since second grade. We had been assigned seats next to each other in fourth-period maths, which we had both failed. She had light-brown gossamer hair, a rosebud mouth set against very fair skin and constantly fiddled with a plain silver band on her right index finger.

Simi was very pretty, and because I was ugly as sin, I had to be her friend.

Her name is an anomaly: Simone Das. On paper she sounds like she speaks a little bit of Bangla with a pronounced Parisian accent. In reality, she speaks flawless Bangla and not a word of French. No one knows why her earthy, staunchly Bengali parents gave her this floaty, foreign name. I like to think it was a moment of whimsy, a shy hand grasped by a tentative paw one week before an arranged marriage. Maybe a character in some book they had both read times over (because when two people—even strangers—discover a book they both have loved, it feels like a shared secret).

Over time, I developed a great fondness for Simi. She was adorable and a fool. Anyone could take advantage of her with the merest show of friendship, and my affection for her grew out of a fierce protectiveness that wanted both to stop her from being so open to hurt and yet never, ever have her change.

Devika's was a destination wedding, a novel concept at the time. Since the facade of upholding communist principles had to be maintained, the destination was in West Bengal itself, at an imposing old British-era fort on the banks of the Ganges. The fort had been converted into a plush five-star hotel by Sunny Arora, the groom's father, but thankfully, the architects, designers, landscapers et al. had been able to resist the urge to stain warm red brick with cold stretches of glass and steel.

The Aroras had rammed all their Punjabi aesthetic into the wedding parties. The fort lay silhouetted against lawns laden with festivities. In a nod to his immense wealth, Sunny Arora had asked that the traditional dhol and shehnai players be supplemented with an international DJ—'from the Europe only, ji.'

All around, everything was awash with the bright fluorescence of lights under a canopy of alternating royal-purple and rani-pink bands. The canopy stretched so far and wide that the eye searched in vain for a single spot of sky. Finding none, it moved down to the party below, where beautiful people moved about like the heartbreaking strains of a violin, resplendent in silk and chiffon and rouge and *polki*. The only breaks in the riot of colours were tables draped in white linen and studded with Baccarat dinnerware, glittering like calm pebbles against an endless shore.

I felt intolerably gauche in my powder-blue Swarovski-studded lehenga. The luxurious fabric swam around me, making me look like an imposter. I was better off in my refuge of jeans and an oversized T-shirt.

'Shoot, Ma's coming.'

Aunty was heading to where Simi and I stood cornering jacketed waiters and clearing out their platters of hors d'oeuvres, ostensibly to drag us off for another round of introductions. I wished again that Button and Cookie had been allowed to attend the wedding.

My family had been loath to let me partake of Debi Mullick's hospitality as well. The politician was a pariah amongst the old order. He had been born into our world, for shame. How greed had led him astray! He had become a follower of Marx, of all the wrong ideas. He had wasted the good blood (Bengali, Brahmin, pure), and that was unforgivable.

In the end, I had been allowed to come only because my parents adored Simi.

'Simi, Tara, come meet Choruji.'

Choruji was Debi Mullick's wife, and my grand-aunt by marriage, thrice removed. She stretched like a corpulent octopus over a large length of a brocade couch, and as Simi's mother ushered me towards her, I had the distinct, uncomfortable, ridiculous notion of feeling like a sacrificial lamb.

Aunty made some unfunny joke about how our families were connected through generations. So sweet that Simi and I had become such good friends, na?

Known for being as sparing with her words as she was extravagant with her diet, Choruji took me in slowly, in detail. I remembered being deathly afraid of her as a child. The expanse of her fat swallowed up her features, and I used to be scared because it looked like she had no face.

Without warning, she grabbed my cheek and gave it a hard pinch.

'Good nose. Still too fat, no?'

I gaped at her. But she was done with me and had moved on to Simi. Her gaze held approval now, and she smiled as she asked her how old we had become.

'Seventeen, Choruji.'

'Too young still, no? Three, four more years, and then we can find you a boy.'

I felt a strong rush of dislike for Choruji. Hate, almost. To be fair, it extended beyond just her. I was holding her up as a representative, symbolic and universal. And I wondered, is this really all people see when they look at other people? A nice nose and bad body? Is this all we could be? And why was this not all I could see?

That old familiar, a great blue sadness, crept up beside me.

I tugged at Simi's mother's sari, the zardozi border pricking points into my skin. 'Aunty, I'm not feeling well. Could I go lie down in my room, please?'

I knew of a little path, largely obscured by untended shrubbery, which led straight down from the lawns where the party was being held to the banks of the Ganges. It was muddy from the high tide, but that damn lehenga had caused me so much grief that I merely rejoiced at the wet earth collecting on my hem.

As I walked, I stopped trying to battle the sadness. I had found that letting it wash over me was therapeutic, in a way.

I am a liar. I am gauche. I am confused. I am seventeen. And I am young. Too young.

At seventeen, we don't realize what it means to be seventeen. We can't quite see the world for what it is, though we've started to feel it a bit. And it gives us, it gives me, a hint of how horribly alone the going will get.

I stood at the bank for a long time. The water had been blue when I got there, but began turning a deep gold as the sun started going down. The bobbing boats dotting the vista seemed to be moving shoreward, heading back home. But I'd been concentrating on what lay past the boats, further down, closer to the horizon, because I was still seventeen and the horizon still looked like freedom.

I would be glad to leave. The wedding, the fort, the city, the country, the home. I wasn't sure which part of it all made me feel like this, foreign in my own skin. But I think it was just that I had started to sense that I wasn't where I was supposed to be. What was I supposed to do, here in the middle of this big fat Gatsby party? Who was I supposed to be? I wasn't like everyone else. Of course, this is not to say that everyone is the same, but they are, at least, some personal version of sane.

All this while, the evening had been stealing away, bringing the night closer and closer. And I'd been staring at the water, the sun dying upon it, spreading as it melted and sank. Burned, and drowned.

I felt quite mad.

Recently, my parents had started staging frequent weekend getaways to this fort-hotel. We spent a lot of time swimming and eating, and when they retired to their room to sleep away the blazing afternoons, my brother and I explored the grounds.

While Polo clambered down to the banks of the river and asked the local kids to teach him how to skip rocks, I walked down to the caretaker's cottage, hoping to get a story and a biscuit out of the wizened old man. He had lots of stories to tell, but I always asked him to repeat the enduring legend surrounding the fort: Caroline's story.

She had been brought here when she was just eleven; her father, Commodore Harringdon, had been stationed at the fort over a hundred years ago, when the Raj still ruled. The river-bound fort was one of the most important British outposts in Eastern India, under constant threat from French forces in the neighbouring district of Chandernagar, and Caroline grew well into her teenage years without ever being able to leave the premises.

In the spring of her sixteenth year, as a fresh new regiment drew into the harbour, relieving those who had served too long under a hot sun, Caroline met Charles.

Caroline and Charles were two of a kind in a strange land, filled with dark, silent people who didn't speak their language. They met every night, up on the highest battlement of the fort, and when it was time for Charles's regiment to head back to England, devised a plan for Caroline to stow away on the ship. As the day of departure approached, though, Caroline grew afraid of the unknown. She told Charles she would stay—here, in this place, a world foreign to her, but still her home.

The story goes that the lovers bid each other a painful adieu and parted ways. As Caroline paced their battlement on that night, a bright light over the river caught her eye. She ran down and across the grounds, past the sandy beach and to the harbour, where the flaming ship was sinking into the water. There were no survivors, and never was anything heard of Caroline again.

Some say that you can see her on certain nights, a long shadow in an old-fashioned dress, her eternal soul still keeping vigil on the shore.

The caretaker, sweet old man that he was, never wearied of repeating the story, but could only do so by rote. I peppered him with questions, thirsting for more details, for more story— what happened to the ship? Why did she run to a sinking ship anyway? Did she burn or did she drown?

'Such strange questions you ask, little girl. No one knows these answers.'

'But you must have searched around, to find out more of what happened! Don't you want to know?'

'Too much curiosity is dangerous, beta,' he would caution, and bribe away further questions with another biscuit.

So I spent a lot of time playing with the story in my mind, filling in gaps, embellishing the contours. On the weekend getaways, I sometimes slipped out of my room late at night to go looking for Caroline. She was the only ghost I had never felt scared of.

Now, I heard footsteps behind me. Someone was walking up the razed path. Reflexes told me to turn around and check that it wasn't some psychopath killer with an axe and a chainsaw. But I felt quite numb, and couldn't exactly move, though I'm not really sure I was even trying.

A déjà voice asked whether he was interrupting me.

I shook my head, no, and hoped he wouldn't try and make small talk.

I cannot take any more small talk. I cannot answer another question about how I know the bride or which grade I'm in. Where was Caroline when you needed her?

'Alas. No signs of a shipwreck.'

Caroline's wreck?

'I'm sorry, what?'

'I heard a nice story about this place. There should be a shipwreck somewhere around here, according to it. Perhaps it was only a myth.'

'Perhaps the wreck you're looking for isn't something you can see.'

His voice was wrinkled with a smile. 'Ah, you know about Caroline's ghost.'

'What happened to the ship?'

'Gunpowder stores blew. The wooden ribs must have washed up on the shore. I think the tide would have showed the skeleton.'

I cracked open a grin. He hadn't missed a beat.

'Why did she follow him in, then?'

This time, he waited so long to answer that I thought he hadn't heard. 'She was trying to save him.'

I felt his presence like a remembrance. As though we had met before, in some other life if not this one. And then felt an almost irrepressible urge to tell him that, though I battled it into a somewhat more socially compliant shape.

'She died, you know.'

He didn't say anything. The sun started browning, folding all the light into the horizon.

Soon it would be dark.

'Sometimes an end is nothing in the face of what has been.'

The lump in my throat stopped short at the catch in his voice.

Unanchored, in a quick, brave, breathless rush I asked the kind of question I had always known not to.

'Are you sad?'

'If there is reason to be.' A fine edge leadened the words. I must have imagined him.

'There is reason to be,' I said, crossing my arms, drawing my body into itself, and looking out over the water, my eyes drifting past the homeward-bound boats.

'Ah, yes. The light.'

Oh.

I nodded. Yes, the light. The melting light. The melting, fading, dying light. The end of day, the end of days. Caroline and her bright young soldier, my endless expanse of teenage time.

And then, propelled by an eruption of giddiness, I said, 'It flew too close to the sun.'

He laughed appreciatively. 'You're a little crazy, aren't you?'
'I feel quite mad.'

Well, then. I'd said that out loud, hadn't I? Odd, how I didn't instantly regret it.

'But of course.' He sounded, in the infinite universe suspended in that infinitesimal moment, deeply sad. 'Dear girl, this is a hurt particular to loving a world that refuses to love you back.'

Something about the way he said 'dear girl' got stuck inside me, and it felt really nice, like a spool of soft, warm wool. So I let it be. I put it away like a prize, carefully, to be taken out and admired and relished on crappy days.

'People like us, we are moved by too much. Even the smallest, most insignificant things. Things that are not really "real". And this becomes a problem, I know.'

He does know, I thought, everything changing. He knows.

'But we must not be afraid of ourselves, dear girl. This is the most beautiful part of us, this hopeless madness filled with too much love. It is bound to drive us a little crazy. But it is, in the end, a fair price to pay for the adventures we shall have.'

After a minute, it occurred to me that I was being rude, staring off into the distance, like I wasn't listening, like I wasn't branding these words into myself, turning them into a part of me.

And I was afraid to turn around and match a face to the voice, afraid with a half-formed fear of never being able to look away. But I looked anyway.

Blitzkrieg.

The tousle of his hair, the pink pooling in the centre of his mouth, the line of his neck as he turned his head towards me—a straight, strong arrow from the lobes of his ears to the collar of his shirt.

The contraction of my heart with the spreading of his smile.

I resorted to the stupid pseudo-philosophy of not being able to think straight. 'So we're cursed, then? We hold ourselves prisoners?'

'Would you like to dance?'

'Now?'

He motioned to the air around. 'It helps with the overwhelming.'

I fumbled for a way to destroy the moment, because really, how do you let something that perfect be?

So, I shrugged. 'There's no music, dude.'

He moved a step closer. We would dance.

Smiling now, I said, 'You're quite mad yourself, you know.'

'Nietzsche, my dear girl.'

'What?'

He laughed and held out his hand, like something out of a movie, like the best scene in the novels I read hidden between pages of textbooks, like the boy who drew Caroline to a burning ship.

'May I?'

He waited till I nodded a nervous yes to take my left hand in his right. Then he put his other hand on the small of my back and silly me, I hadn't noticed—the music was in the movements. It had been there all along.

He began humming a tune as we started moving. Locked in the space between his arms and a buttoned expanse of Wedgwood blue, I could suddenly smell his aftershave, a scent that I vaguely remembered loving as a child. We were dancing

a waltz before I could think another thought. Viennese, as I
would find out later. Well, he was dancing the Viennese waltz,
anyway. I was merely moving to his ebb and flow.

Whatever he was humming sounded familiar.

'Where is this from?' Somewhere in the back of my mind,
I was surprised that I had spoken.

He looked past my shoulder and whispered in my ear,
'Why, it's the waltz from *The Godfather*.'

The humming had stopped, but my body was already used to
the rhythm; three beats, a turn, one way, then another. I tried to
imagine myself not quite as me; prettier, surer, dancing the song
along a wide castle ballroom, a princess chosen by the prince . . .
some scene from a movie watched and forgotten long ago.

'Do you know, this is the first time I've danced with someone
whose name I don't know.'

'Tara. Well, Nayantara, but that's too many syllables.'

'Well then, what do we do about Vijay?'

'Jay?'

'Jay it is.'

He blinked for a second, and I realized I had been in a
staring contest with him. With the blink, my foot seemed
to pause of its own accord, tripping me up, throwing me
headlong into the final inches of his arms, pushing my chest
up against his.

I stumbled back, only to find his hand still there, steadying
me. He pretended as though nothing had happened. As if my
momentary loss of faith in our brief encounter was but an
expected result of it. Gingerly, I held my breath, willing the
moment not to end, never to end. But an hour or a second in,
he gently took us apart.

He smiled at me, and I felt a welling panic rise in sharp little bumps all down my arms and legs.

'We should head back to the party. Someone must be looking for you.'

It was hurt and it was glue, his assumption that I mattered, that I would be missed. I knew something was happening to me then. I had just been introduced to the feeling that I would measure everyone else against.

I shook my head. 'I think I'll stay here a while longer.'

In the distance, I heard the party drawing to a crescendo. They started sending up fireworks, blowing up the sky. He turned to leave, but took a second to look back, smile and say, *'And those who were seen dancing were thought to be insane by those who could not hear the music.'*

*5 January 2008*

# Rio

### Vijay Dhillon
### 9810000001

I flipped around to the back of the card, looking for anything else at all. There was nothing. That was it. Just his name and an expensive number.

Should I call? He had said I could, but what if he was just being polite? It hadn't seemed like he was. Quite the opposite, in fact; his words had a pared deliberation to them, a heaviness I could almost hold.

Making a concentrated effort to keep my fingers from shaking, I dialled Jay's number. In my head, I had practised our conversation several times over.

'Hi.'

'Hi. Who is this?'

'I wanted to wish you a happy new year.' I would smile while I said this, so he could hear it in my voice.

'Ah, Tara. How are you?'

'I feel strangely inclined to share a secret with you.'

'What is it?'

'I want to own everyone in the world.'

I left it at that. If our previous meeting was anything to go by, his reality would supersede my imagination. In his response, I knew, there would somehow be answers to questions I hadn't known how to ask.

At the first ring, I got up and started pacing, unable to sit still.

Abruptly, the ringing stopped. Had he cut the call? No, he wouldn't do that. Why would he do that? Already adrenalized, I called again. This time, the phone rang only once, and then all I could hear was a rhythmically pounding sort of sound, dissonant and laden with static. It was loud enough that I could feel the speaker held up to my ear vibrate to its beat.

'H-hello?'

'Hello? Who is this?'

I could barely hear him over the pounding sound.

'Hi, I—'

'Hey, I'm in Rio. Can't hear a thing. Can I call you back?'

I clicked off the phone without responding. He sounded so different from the boy outside the wedding. Short. Clipped. Matter-of-fact. Normal, really. A sexy-voiced normal, of course, but quite unlike the ephemeral presence at the water's edge.

Though this was the first time I had ever thought the word 'sexy' in association with a real, living person. It was reserved for pop stars and actors, wasn't it? Tom Cruise and Nick Carter were sexy, not real live boys. Real live boys were like the badly shaven specimens milling around outside my brother's school grounds as Button and I waited in the car to pick him up. Lumbering and awkward, talking about cricket with their mouths full of Uncle Chips and Perk bars.

Maybe I *had* just imagined him after all.

## Milka

'I called Jay last night.'

'And you waited till now to tell me?'

Button and I had landed up at Cookie's place after school, inviting ourselves over for what would definitely be a delicious lunch. Far beyond behaving like guests, we were sprawled side by side on Cookie's bed while she chatted with her mum in the kitchen.

Even though their large house was crawling with maids and cooks and cleaners and chauffeurs, Aunty insisted on doing all the cooking herself, to everyone's delight; she was one of that rare breed who could whip even abhorrent things like vegetables into delicacies. Every day, Uncle would take a break from presiding over his archipelago of companies—matchsticks, acres of prime real estate and prawn farms—to come home and have lunch with his wife and daughter.

'Button, it was really bad.'

'What happened?'

'I hung up without saying anything.'

Button propped herself up on her elbows and glared at me. 'Why?'

'Well, he couldn't really hear, and—I don't know. It just felt stupid. To have called, I mean. He doesn't have space for me in his life.'

'You don't know that.'

I shrugged, then got up and ambled over to Cookie's dresser, peering gloomily at myself in the mirror.

Button came up behind me and pulled a face at her reflection. 'Just look at my hair.'

'Dude, please. Just look at mine.'

She glanced over at me. 'Yeah.'

I snorted. 'Bitch.'

She laughed and flopped back on the bed.

Sighing, I sat down next to her.

'He was at some party-sounding thing in Rio.'

'Where's that?'

'Brazil.'

She whistled. 'He lives a cool life.'

'Yeah.'

Cookie came into the room. 'Oi, lunch is served. Get your lazy asses off the bed.'

'In a minute,' Button mumbled, digging her face into a fluffy pillow.

I groaned off the bed and draped myself around Cookie in a full-body hug. 'Hi, Cooks!'

'Get off me, you freak.'

I nuzzled her ear. 'But I *loooove* you!'

She broke into reluctant tickle-induced giggles and swatted at me with her tiny hands. 'Oof, stop! Come eat.'

Laughing, I got off her and pulled the pillow out from under Button's head. 'Yeah, let's.'

Uncle broke into a smile as the three of us entered the dining room.

'Hi, Uncle,' Button said, sliding into a chair.

'We've invited ourselves over again, as you can see,' I added, dropping into a seat beside her.

'Good. I'm glad.'

'Stop encouraging them, Baba. I already see more of these two than I want to.'

'You're not very nice to your friends,' Aunty remarked, passing around the salad. Thoroughly enticed by the steaming bowls of chicken and lamb on the table, I passed it to Button without so much as touching the serving handle. She reluctantly put a cucumber and a single piece of lettuce on her plate. One of the maids caught me eyeing the chicken and made a move to start serving it.

Aunty stopped her. 'Hold on, dear. Not till she eats some vegetables first.'

'But, but, Aunty! Must I?'

She spooned a generous helping of salad on to my plate in response.

Uncle chuckled over his bowl of gazpacho. 'The things we have to go through to get to the meat!'

'Keep space for dessert, all of you. I've made chocolate mousse,' Aunty said. Button and I let out loud whoops of joy.

Conversation turned to our plans for college. Uncle and Aunty wanted to know whether I'd decided on anything yet. I told them that I'd whittled down a list of places, but that the admission procedures would take close to six months. Only one thing was set in stone: I was going to America.

It was almost de rigueur for girls from The House to leave the country for a few years post high school, graduate classes scattered around the world and bring back art history and English degrees as proud souvenirs. A select few dispensed with the pretentions and went straight to Saks and Selfridges instead, getting a head start on putting together a perfect trousseau.

A maid brought out dessert. I felt like I could have eaten the entire mass of chocolate myself, but a memory of the image in Cookie's mirror restrained me to a small dollop.

'Don't you want some more?' Button asked, already on her second helping. Morosely, I shook my head.

'You should talk some sense into your friend.' Uncle turned to me. 'I've been telling Imon to go abroad, to go wherever she wants, but she seems stuck on staying here.'

Cookie calmly ate another spoon of mousse. 'I'm not leaving home yet, Baba. But I'll think about it for my Masters.'

'Me neither,' said Button, finishing off the last of the mousse at a rate that was equal parts alarming and amusing.

'Well, I for one am very happy to hear that,' said Aunty. 'It's bad enough to think of Tara leaving.'

Button snorted. 'Aunty, don't be so polite. You know it'll be a relief to get rid of this baboon.'

I stuck my tongue out at her. 'You're just jealous because Aunty loves me more. And we should get going. I have to be home before The Wolf gets mad.'

Uncle walked us to the door. As I was leaving, he slipped a thick bar of Milka into my hand. It was my favourite kind of chocolate, saccharine and a rare treat unavailable on Indian shores.

'You're too young to start denying yourself the things that make you happy, kid.'

I grinned and gave him a hug, going home comforted by Aunty's food and Uncle's gentle existence, enveloped in the warm glow of Cookie's happy family.

————

That night, after several unsuccessful attempts at studying for a political science exam, I collapsed on my favourite seat by the window in my bedroom, reliving the disastrous call to Jay for the hundredth time. Glumly, I acknowledged the fact that I could never call him again after that. Could I? Should I?

Button's immediate opinion on the matter was required. I picked up my phone to call her, and started as it began vibrating in my hand, flashing a number on the little green screen.

9810000001

Fuck.

I answered.

'Hey! Did you call me?'

FUCK.

'Um, yeah, sorry about that.'

He laughed. My stomach turned.

'Unnecessary apology. Tara, right? What's up?'

'Oh, I—it wasn't anything specific. Nothing really, you must be busy, I'll catch you later!'

'I'm free now. Tell me.'

I felt some combination of embarrassed and indebted, but not in a terrible way.

'Well, it's nothing important. I just wanted to talk to someone.'

'All right. Let's talk. How was your new year's eve?'

'Quiet. Not at all like Rio must have been.'

He laughed again. 'Patience, dear girl. You'll get there. How old are you?'

'Seventeen.'

'Mm, go before you're twenty-one.'

'Why?'

'Some things are just better experienced in the first flush of adulthood.'

'How so?'

'You'll see. By the way, have you read any Nabokov?'

'I've read *Lolita*.'

'Really?'

'Yeah. Why?'

'I'm pleasantly surprised.'

'Why?'

'And curious. What did you think of it?'

'The writing was brilliant.'

'And?'

I sighed. 'I felt very bad for Humbert.'

He was laughing again. 'Good.'

'What is?'

'Reading things all wrong.'

Was I irritated or thrilled, amused or intrigued? They cast a strange balance together, and my voice was steady, bereft of inflection, when I said, 'Why do you never give straight answers?'

'Good question.'

'See!'

'Have you watched *Dead Poets Society*?'

'Nope. Should I?'

'You should. Right away, in fact. What's your email address?'

'juvenile_delinquent89@hotmail.com'

'That's a ridiculous address. Aren't you applying to colleges soon?'

It had not occurred to me how unprofessional that sounded. 'Yeah. I need to change it, don't I?'

'Check your inbox in ten minutes. I'm sending you a link to Gmail and *Dead Poets Society*. Set up an account with your name in it—no frills—and then reward yourself with the movie.'

Disappointment washed over me. Was he going to go?

'Are you going?'

'Need to sleep, love. Have to make a flight in five hours.'

'Oh, okay. Where to?'

'New York.'

'Fun!'

There was a long pause. I was about to check the line when he said, 'Something like that. Good night, dear girl.'

Abuzz from the conversation, I went and turned on my computer. Eight minutes of Minesweeper later, I checked my inbox and found an email from Jay titled:

The straight answer is rarely ever the
right one.

We listened to a lot of the soul wrenchers, a lot of Coldplay and the moments when it was just Axl and a bottle of scotch and his fingers turning the piano red. Paradoxes and repetitions; we learned the language, we learned their tongues. Shaggy-haired Jon Bon Jovi on his bed of nails, not alone but still lonely, and Chris Martin, his eyes so blue, never having been told it was easy, never having been told it would be this hard. I'll take you back to the start.

## Stems

I was in the wrong classroom on my first day of school.

The teacher read through her register, and my name wasn't called out. I raised my hand, squeaked out my name. She flipped through the register and told me that I was in the wrong room. Then she went out into the hallway and came in with a tall, thin senior and instructed her to get me to the KG-2 classroom.

The senior looked down at me, and I wanted to get to know her. But she was a senior, she was tall and thin and looked like she lived in Alipore. After leading me through what seem to be endless passages, she handed me over to another senior, a curly-haired girl with thick glasses. 'Oi, I'm late for chem lab again. Take this one to KG-2.'

I noticed that I didn't seem to know a lot of basic things. Things the other girls all knew. Things like not looking out of the window in class (but I had been listening, Ma'am) and that I should wear a slip under the semi-transparent white tunic of our uniforms. And this made no sense to me, because I also knew that I was smart. 'Full of potential,' as the teachers kept telling my parents. 'But she doesn't pay attention. Where is her mind?'

———

I grew up in a sprawling old house on a tea-stained street in North Calcutta. It was nuts in there; people everywhere, family and servants and those who had blurred the line between the two so long ago that they were just there—in the rooms that led out from and into one another, and at the *luchi*-topped table stretching across a vast dining hall.

We kept a cow in the garage, for milk and cream, and a mad aunt up on the empty third floor. She had small hands and smaller feet and threw furniture around if her tightly plotted day got thrown off schedule. She counted time—four minutes of walking, eight in the bath. Six minutes of tea and nine for prayer at six in the evening. The nurses never stayed for long.

Sometimes, in her eyes, I could see my life like a bridge, unfurling ahead of me and behind me, a largedarkhulk. I panicked. I was scared—I am scared—the juices inside the womb I swam about in had cooked me all wrong, hadn't they? I could see it, I could see into her brain through her manic eyes and they were mine, I looked like that inside, and I was barely six and I knew this would be my secret to fight, to carry, for the rest of my life. I had seen it before, peeking out from inside my mother's pregnant stomach, using her distended belly button as a peephole. I saw it again, I saw it all—this, the past, dense. Where I came from. The people as they were, before age started fading them away into the general shape of adults. I saw what was and will always be inside me as I bubbled to life inside a warm, wet water balloon of a cave.

I saw the *didas* and the *kakas* and the *pishis* and their kids. I saw my grandfather, roaring into the house after rounds at the hospital like an angered wolf. And Aunty Agnes, a retired old nurse adopted into the family by him.

Aunty Agnes was constantly angry and tired, always brittle and sharp. She spent a lot of time watching television soap operas, and when she wasn't doing that, she sat on her bed and stared at the birds she kept in a big cage in the balcony.

They said it was because she never got married. Some said she was unfortunate. Others, like my Uncle Shri, said she didn't try hard enough. But they all agreed that if she had been married, had a normal life and a man to take care of her, she would have been happy.

By the time I was old enough to see the world through eyes unclouded by confused wonder, I had a baby brother named Polo, the family had broken apart; The Wolf and my parents had moved us to a long, white house in quiet, leafy south Calcutta. I turned six, and spent the mornings trying to fake fevers by willing my skin hot, not wanting to leave the comfort of bed to zip past a slumbering city to The House.

I read *Archie Comics* and *Sweet Valley High* and watched a lot of American sitcoms from the eighties. The only television show that was streamed in India relatively at the same time as it was in America was *Friends*. It ran only a couple of seasons behind and we all tried to schedule our post-school tutorials in a way that allowed us to be home at six every weekday evening. Everyone was devastated when the show ended. I didn't watch the last episode.

Shortly before the turn of the millennium, my dad brought home what looked like a big white TV. It didn't play any shows, so I mostly just ignored it, letting Polo play car-racing games on it all day. But then a little black box was attached to it, and everything else became boring, inconsequential.

This wasn't like watching grown-ups drink coffee somewhere along the mythical streets of New York City. These were real people, real girls my age living in the suburbs of Cleveland and Baltimore.

I learnt to want: a little white girl, with the hair and the skin that made people pretty, the comforter-covered bed in the pink room and the parents who let her stay out late, and the blonde Backstreet-like boys who she had access to, could talk to, who would fall over themselves to talk to her.

Who had that television-screen life? What kind of person are you? How do we even inhabit the same planet? We are the same, isn't that what everybody says? I covet what it means to be you, and because you are the converse of everything I am, where does that leave me?

They were just ideas in my head; mirages, almost. And yet, every so often, I couldn't help that they controlled me.

Sometimes, it just felt like my bones were cracking apart. Like this shell that holds the mass of who I am broke right open, threw out all my small thoughts, all the revulsion toward my reality and the guilt—because how could there not be guilt when this was how I felt? How could I sit there and just feel unhappy by comparing the lives we were born into? That never felt right, but it was. It just was.

Still, I would not be helpless, so I just bent down on my broken knees and used my creaking arms to stuff the whole mess right back inside. I swelled up like a suitcase whose neatly folded contents had been thrown back in, worn and crumpled. I ate a sleeve of chocolate cookies, and two sleeves of the ones with the smiley faces on them. The vanilla cream inside bulged out of the eyes and the sugary smile on the cookie, so I licked the cream out of those first and then bit into the three layers of cheer-up. Cookie, cream, cookie.

———————

I met those unicorns sometimes. I saw them on the holidays my parents took us on every few months, to resorts on the beach and city rooms with cloud-like beds. That was the only time we spent together as a family. I was always amazed when classmates worried about what a mother would say about an ink stain on a uniform or how a father would rage about a bad grade. My parents were almost never at home. I saw them rarely, at dinner, three or four times a week. It seemed so strange to me that there were mothers who saw what state their children came home in, who cooked lunch for them and knew what they were studying in class, or fathers who looked into their school books to check what grades they'd received. It seemed like an incredible, delicious violation of privacy, and I longed to be able to grouse about it with friends.

At those holiday family dinners, Polo and I would eat till we wanted to throw up. My mother would worry a little but my dad would just laugh and tell us about the time he and a friend hunted, roasted and ate an entire lamb. He'd call for another scotch and tell us about his work trying to identify strains of HIV in a remote northern village back when he was a scientist for the government, before he built the factory where sweaty men loaded steel rods into big, whirring machines. I'd stop eating when he'd describe carrying pails of infected blood by hand—'precious research material, we couldn't leave it behind'—when their van broke down in the middle of a deserted countryside, and worry about it for the rest of the trip. When the waiters came to clear our plates, he'd tell them to wait till we got the cutlery placement just right. We'd straighten our forks and make sure that our knife edges faced inwards, angling them both to five o'clock.

I preferred these short family vacations, filled with unicorns and their stories, than the longer summer ones when Polo and I were shipped off to Delhi to spend time with my mom's side of the family.

During the days, when my parents would be napping and my brother would be conducting a brisk beachside trade in Pokemon cards, I'd linger around the unicorns, haunt spaces near vacationing families. I talked to them, sometimes, but it was only rarely that I could think of something perfect to say. Mostly, I would just watch them till my mother came and got me from the beach or pool.

You could always tell which ones were the Americans, because they had a lot of things with them. A profusion of caps and creams and toys and sweaters and stuffed animals— an army of things to battle the slightest sign of sun or cold or boredom.

I befriended a Sally for a day, on a beach in Goa. She was building a 'sand-house' ('because castles are for princesses and I want to save the whales') and the freckles across her nose got darker as the day wore on. She didn't like the Backstreet Boys, but she had a pinging, beeping keychain-toy that she let me play with.

'It's a tamagotchi pet. You have to keep it alive, okay?'

———

It was time for fifth grade, and again, I was in the wrong classroom.

Mrs Gupta read out names from the register and, shaking her head, led me to the class next door. I was embarrassed, but went largely unnoticed because of the general chaos ensuing as teachers configured their classroom seating arrangements, shuffling the students around to maximize attentiveness.

I was told to take a seat in the front row, next to Atreyi Thakur. I didn't know her personally, but I knew that she was best friends with Imon Majumdar, who travelled abroad frequently and was a repository of cool stationery and Toblerone bars (that only a lucky few got to partake of). They were the leaders of an unbroachable group and occupied the benches next to the sweet shop at recess.

While Mrs Lewis was writing down important dates from the Battle of Waterloo on the blackboard, I studied the portrait of a stocky little man in the World History textbook. 'Napoleon had a really big bum.'

Next to me, Button laughed out loud.

Mrs Lewis turned around. 'And what do we find so amusing, Atreyi?'

———

I wanted to be best friends with Button very badly. She was as fascinating to me as the unicorns, and that was an interesting turn of events.

# Shamiana

I was on my knees in the hallway, crawling from the XII Commerce classroom to the Humanities room opposite.

'Nayantara, exactly *what* is it you're doing?'

Shit. It was The Raccoon. Nicknamed after the giant dark circles that seemed to encompass the entire middle section of her face, The Raccoon was a history and civil studies teacher and, thankfully for me, rather wispy, both of body and mind. She would float into class in an unravelling sari and giant red beads on her ears and neck, deliver a forty-five-minute lecture on the demerits of socialism and float back out. We would then collectively snap shut our Indian history textbooks and, depending on the level of individual investment in excelling the upcoming ISC exams, bitterly complain or hysterically laugh. Of course, we could have interrupted her and told her she was teaching the wrong class, but the faultlessly polite young ladies of The House never corrected their teachers.

Looking back, it is distinctly possible that The Raccoon was blazed out of her mind through most of her classes.

Still, she couldn't fail to notice the rotund, mop-topped

blue-and-white figure trawling about on the ground in an otherwise deserted corridor.

'I fell?'

Even as I said it, I felt the plausibility of my statement being called into question. This was in part because I had been caught mid-crawl, yes, but the sizeable chunk of spicy chicken chop in my mouth was largely to blame.

I had been sitting on the floor in the back of the huge Commerce classroom—where old, half-blind Mrs Chopra was writing copious notes on Microeconomic theory on the chalkboard—and stealing bits of the delicious lunch Aunty had packed for Cookie. She ignored me almost completely as I ransacked her lunch box, laboriously taking notes and only occasionally smacking my head when I made too much noise.

Now, to buy time, I clutched at the voluminous folds of my Catholic skirt and said, 'Ow. My leg.'

The Raccoon stared at me with large, raccoony eyes.

The floor was the cold, hard stone that all pre-Independence British Raj buildings seem to be made of, and my knees were starting to hurt.

'I think you should get up and go into class.'

'Yes, ma'am,' I mumbled around the chicken chop.

She walked in through the door at the head of the classroom and, chewing furiously, I bolted in through the back.

Simultaneously swallowing and sliding into the seat next to Button, I hissed, 'She saw me crawling in here with half of Cookie's tiffin in my mouth.'

Button made a sort of gurgling, squealing sound and disappeared behind *The Rise and Fall of Western Political Ideologies of the Twentieth Century*. Behind Alexander Shittles's homicidal tome (a hideously dull text rumoured to have lulled many a student into death by boredom), she shook and wept.

On the blackboard, The Raccoon started detailing the structure of village panchayats prevalent in the interiors of India.

I grabbed a notebook and scribbled furiously—*If you don't stop laughing she's going to chuck us out of class, you bleeding goat.*

Button nodded, but continued to shake into the textbook.

Sreemoyee Das turned around to shoot us a dirty look from the row ahead. She usually sat in the first row, but the other geeks had filled up the front half of the room before she got into class that day. Detained by whatever nonsense pursuit she had been caught up in (probably begging for a physics test or something, the cow), Sreemoyee had been forced to sit in one of the back rows, which were always the last to fill up because everyone knew that's where the bad girls sat.

To be fair, Sreemoyee did grow up to be a civil studies teacher herself, so I guess being able to concentrate in that class really was important to her. Then, however, I just flipped off the back of her oily, braided head and Button kept up her tickled convulsions.

I was convinced that we were going to be told to leave the room and go down to the vice principal's office. Not that I really minded getting into trouble. That happened too often for me to go into a panic over, as most of the good girls of The House did if ever they were caught with a cell phone or some forbidden lip gloss on school grounds. But there were two big reasons that made me very reluctant to break The Raccoon's patience.

For one, I loved the vice principal. Dr Roshan was one of

those people who're born to play exactly the role they do. An excellent administrator, with smartly cropped hair and the eternal soul of a teacher, she dressed starchily and spoke crisply, in deliberated, weighty sentences. She visibly winced when students mispronounced words, and paused whatever she was doing to explain in a patient, pained voice exactly why it was 'too-ih-shun' and not 'tew-shun'.

In Dr Roshan, Button and I fancied a kindred spirit some half a century thence. And seeing the disappointment in her eyes every time we were sent down to her office was worse than whatever was meted out as the actual punishment. More often than not, it was just detention, but—and this is the second reason—sometimes parents were given a call and told to come in the next day to discuss the terrible human being that their child was obviously developing into. This didn't matter much to me, since my parents were usually out of town on work, inadvertently giving me a free pass (a very strongly worded note that I would forge a signature on). But Button's parents were a whole different story. Well, mostly just her mum, who would ground her till the next year if she spoke to one of these infuriated teachers. Considering that Button lived in a state of semi-grounding anyway—no unsupervised television, phone privileges or going out after school hours—this was, to say the least, very, very undesirable. We already spent half our time trying to lie our way around the semi-grounding. A high-alert, airtight grounding scenario would be nigh insurmountable.

This time, The Raccoon fortunately chose to ignore the heaving figure of Button behind Shittles's book. Though I think that was probably just because she was twenty minutes late for class—effectively having prompted me herself, really, to crawl next door in boredom and in search of food—and didn't want to waste any more time.

I took this show of leniency as a sign to continue disregarding the ongoing lecture and continued to write to Button in the Bitching Book.

Cookie said she heard Riddhi's going to make a poster with Kage's name on it and take it to Shamiana with her!

Dude, are you serious? I'm actually embarrassed for her. Which is saying something, considering how despo she always is.

Flossy said he walked super late into some class last week and said it was because a monkey tried to attack him on the way. Apparently it was a substitute teacher and she was so freaked out that she actually left the class and went down to the office to sound an alarm.

Well, that's kind of funny, I guess. But he really, really likes to be the centre of attention, doesn't he?

Yeah, obviously. He's the only one who does all those theatrics at Shamiana.

Should make for a good show, though.

Yeah, hopefully. He better not ruin any Bon Jovi songs.

Can you imagine if we pulled the monkey stunt in Ugly Bitch's class? Should we?

Yeah, and have her call our mums in again. Fool.

Fine, fine. What time should I pick you up?

Kage was a legend. Among the small clique of private schools that formed our community, Kage was the pinnacle of cool, our very own shaggy-haired, sooty-eyed rock star. He was an irresistible combination of talent and irreverence that had all the girls vying for him. The ones who stood a chance, anyway. The rest of us just talked about him. A lot.

Button and I talked about how we didn't really buy it. He felt like an act. Sure, he had that alluringly messed-up thing going for him—rumour had it, because his parents were in the middle of a nasty divorce—and by all accounts, he could give most professional singers and guitarists a run for their money, but we figured he was too popular to be authentic.

Will come home with you after school. Mum thinks I'm going for the creative writing competition, remember? If she sees me come home and you picking me up, she'll wonder why the school didn't provide transportation.

Cool. I told Budhon Da to make biryani for lunch.

Awesome. And listen, you better actually win the creative writing thing tomorrow. My mum will suspect something if I don't bring home a certificate to show her. But where the hell am I going to get a participation cert with my name on it? You win a medal and I'll distract her with that.

So no pressure.

Lots of pressure. My neck's on the line, that much pressure.

Shit. Not good.

Just win.

Shamiana is the highlight of the school year. We wait for that giant orange-and-blue canopy to be glimpsed above those forbidden grounds, for the old iron gates to be opened up to us. Open up, open up, let us in, we want to let you—*shhhh*.

We have these fests, and the chosen schools pit against each other over four heady days. The best of us are determined by picks and lots, teachers' favourites, and chance and luck. And we're sent off to learn about healthy competition. But we are too young; we thirst for glory, not lessons. For a variety of reasons, ranging from pedestrian desires to please parents, to utilitarian needs to save our skins, we throw healthy competition to the winds and fiercely play, write, click, paint, sing, dance to win. We need to know we're going somewhere. We want to win to predict the future.

And we want to mingle with the other, forbidden, sex. The boys will take their chances with the prettiest skirts, jubilate success and blame failure, and we—well, we will look. At those boys, those boys in uniform. Uniforms that counterpoint ours. Hot blue-and-white linen, stripes, loosened ties. We're separated; our worlds are twined silver cages.

Time to open up the cages—let us out, see what happens.

———

After school, Button and I irritated the chauffeur by playing Aerosmith's *Greatest Hits* CD at a resounding volume. He turned it down after ten minutes with an angry grunt. We glanced at each other but didn't say anything. Crabby old Groucho was perfectly capable of snitching to The Wolf, and that meant a knee-knocking shout reprimanding us for behaving like 'nouveau-riche young brats'. My grandfather, who never loosened his tie before bedtime, reserved the accusation of acting 'nouveau riche' as the master grenade in his impressive arsenal of put-downs.

Stuck in parked traffic outside my brother's school, Groucho said he was going to go look for Polo and got himself the hell away from Steven Tyler.

Calcutta has never been very big on demarcated parking space. Cars settled themselves in wherever they could and waited with the lazy patience of true Bengalis. It sometimes took hours to get out after they had been jammed in by the spontaneous parking lots that invariably formed around busy ports of education, but the languorous nature of life in Marxist Bengal made that de rigueur.

Alone together in the car, Button and I turned the music back up.

*Janie's got a gun . . . BANG!'* we shouted, thumping at the windows. '*Her whole world's come undone . . . BANG!'*

Boys in uniform, of all ages, stared at us as they passed the car. But we didn't care. This was Brothers of the Divine Cross, not St Jude's. BDC was the academic king of Calcutta's closed ring of private schools, true, but it was also home to nerdy boys, with hair parted down the middle and a remarkable proclivity towards pimples and pit stains.

Polo slid into the front passenger seat, turning down the music at once.

Immediately, I donned the mantle requisite of an older sister. 'Why does it take you an hour after school gives out to get out, huh?'

'You're just in a hurry to get to Shamiana and stare at boys.'

'How do you even know about Shamiana, stupid kid?'

'You're the one who's stupid because obviously we see the big boys missing classes for rehearsals and stuff, don't we?'

Button asked, 'What're they playing, do you know?'

'Of course I do.'

I snorted. 'Liar.'

'They're singing "Bed of Roses". I heard them practising during recess.'

Button spent the rest of the ride home raging about wormy BDC boys thinking they could take on the Gods of Rock. I pointed out that Bon Jovi was really just pop/rock, at best, and she punched a red dent into my arm.

———

At my house, we crept past the second floor, where we hoped The Wolf was taking his afternoon nap. If he chanced upon us, we were sure he would know, with all the instinct of a perennially victorious General, that we were a fraction of an inch away from toeing the line. Up on the third floor, I flung down my incongruous Nike backpack and jammed the intercom to bellow for lunch. Then I fought to get in a few bites of the biryani between Polo and Button, who attacked the steaming serving bowl like marauders, forgoing cutlery, plates and civility.

'You're done. We're getting late.' I grabbed the panting Button's arm as she started to dive into the bowl again and dragged her into my room.

Polo followed us in, yelping and looking away as we changed into our good bras and got one of the grinning maids to iron the creases out of our uniforms.

'The boys will see you today, yes?' she said, smoothing my skirt with a hot flick of her hand.

'*Na go.*' Not a chance.

Upon instruction, she slathered a clear layer of glitter polish on to my nails. Button jammed on her favourite headband. Not sure how much perfume to spray on, we drenched ourselves in a dark green bottle of Dior I'd stolen from my mother's heavily laden dressing table.

I glared at the fried dumpling in the mirror. 'I look like shit, Button.'

'You both look like shit.'

'Polo, get the fuck out of my room or I'll tell Mom you were looking at porn on my computer.'

'I wasn't!'

'So?'

'You're a fucking bitch.'

'And you're an annoying little dick, but we all have our cross to bear. Now get out.'

Button locked the door behind him. 'You're so mean to him.'

'I think he has a crush on you.'

'DO NOT!'

I yanked the door open and kicked him somewhere in the region of his balls. Howling retribution, he hobbled away.

'Dude!'

'What?'

'You're going to break his—you know—' she gestured in the general direction of her legs, 'his reproductive thingies!'

'Please, he's a kid. He doesn't need reproductive thingies. Tell me what to do about this!' I jabbed at the ugly mirror.

Button stared at both of us in it and sighed.

The problem was that sometimes, like now, we felt like the real girls, but we never got to look like them.

———

The grounds of St Jude's were electric with the expectation of debutante hormones. People constantly moved in and around the main orange-and-blue shamiana and there was a smorgasbord of uniforms milling all over the grounds, sometimes disappearing in pairs and fours; make-outs for the pretty, while the pimpled and pudgy stood guard as lookouts.

Around five in the evening, the entire assembly congregated inside the shamiana, heating up the place with bodies and anticipation. Western Music was about to begin. Kage was about to perform.

Button and I couldn't stop laughing at the tittering girls who were acting like Bono was about to perform.

But when he came on (at last!), when he prowled down the stage steps and through the aisles, when the shamiana's lights were all turned off save the pool of light trailing a few feet behind him, we could not deny his presence—the languid power of the dark shape outstripping the spotlight. When a thousand voices rose in hoarse unison, bellowing his name to forge some sort of connect with him, we found ourselves hooting right along.

The band behind him played him a fantastic accompaniment to no one's notice.

First, he growled out 'Fear of the Dark', and every sweaty, bespectacled boy raised his own hands and screamed the words, till the giant tent reverberated with the attempts of so many to be some fraction of Kage. Then,

*Now as you close your eyes / Know I'll be thinking about you*

'Bed of Roses'. Jon Bon Jovi at his best. The sound of a thousand wet summer nights around the world.

St Jude's won, of course. There might have been an uprising if they hadn't.

———

It was past eight and Button's parents had been calling on the emergency cell phone she was given when contingencies—like leaving the house after school—arose. Everyone was still busy cheering at the stage left ablaze and empty by Kage, unwilling to let the interlude end. We picked our way out of the shamiana and the school grounds, leaving behind the sounds of the crowd calling for an encore. It was quiet outside, and Button moved into a corner to return the call and complain about the insane traffic holding us up.

Bored, I pulled out my new phone. I was fascinated by it. The screen had a colour display and enough inbuilt memory space to store up to ten of my favourite songs.

'No, Mum, I'm telling you, it's packed outside Jude's. We've been stuck here for twenty minutes!'

Button seemed to be having trouble convincing her parents. We were just *boiled* if they happened to be out on the roads themselves.

Trying not to panic, I hit play on a calming song—*Afraid that what I'll say comes out somehow awry . . .*

'Great band.'

I jumped at the unexpected sound, then stifled an expletive as Kage stubbed his cigarette out. For a second, I just stared at the black loafer grinding the squashed bud on the black, cracked pavement.

Bending, he pulled another cigarette out from the rolled bottom of his trouser leg.

'Smoke?'

I shook my head.

Shrugging, he wet the tip of the filter with his tongue, fired it up with a bright-yellow lighter and took a deep, long drag.

I watched the swirling cloud of smoke for a minute, before he spoke again. 'Hi, by the way. I'm Kage.'

'You are, aren't you? 'Tara. Well, Nayantara, but no one calls me that.'

The song ended. He said, 'Have you heard their new album? It's amazing.'

Be cool, be cool. 'Nope. I'll have to check it out, then.'

'Where do you live? I'll bring it over.'

'Really? I mean, won't your parents mind?'

He shrugged. 'I drive.'

———

Western Music had inaugurated Shamiana with a bang. St Jude's deposited ninety points into their coffers for winning it, and everyone was looking to beat the fast favourites over the course of the next few days. Of course, the other events— lesser things, like writing and photography, collaging and math contests—didn't carry as much weight; points out of twenty, groupies never above zero. But there were lots of them, collectively adding up to three hundred points. We could all perpetrate the lie that every school still had a shot; Shamiana was anyone's to win. It would all come to an end with the dance competition on the last day, another hundred-point battle that would take place under rented strobes to the foreign, fascinating sounds of Ibiza anthems that only the cool kids knew about. Watching the dancers move to Oakenfold in synchronized beats and fluid jerks, their bones like water, was the first time a lot of us got that heady, smoky feeling we'd come to recognize as Friday night after nine rounds in a few years. That stage boils the blood of a generation straight into the pounding heart of clubs.

I took to the lesser glory of my stage—a dank classroom on the third floor of a building on the edge of the grounds. The room bore the faint aroma of a dozen kids who spent all their time inside books, climbing six flights of steep stairs.

Some bespectacled member of our ilk distributed foolscap sheets, and an older lady, probably a teacher, came in and wrote down the topic on the blackboard.

**Write a thoughtfully constructed creative piece on how you would make India a better place, in 2000 words or less.**
**Time remaining: 2 hours**

I couldn't think of anything. This was supposed to be a creative writing competition; the fuck was this Miss World-esque topic?

Bespectacled hands around me were flying across foolscap. I dozed off for a while.

Suddenly, somewhere in the middle of a half-dream where Kage and Button were hatching a plot to steal The Raccoon's red necklace, it hit me—we could just ask Billie to lend her medal. She was sure to win one for Arts & Crafts. No one else in the city could quite turn construction paper into living things the way she did. I sat back, willing her to win, somewhere across the hall.

The teacher lady came back, erased something on the board and filled it in again.

### Time remaining: 35 minutes

Shit.

Okay, it was time to bust something out.

*Nayantara, Mullick*
*The House*
*17 June 2008*

*I have heard it said, in a Voice that is present*
*That holds authority in a vice, that wields truth like a knife,*
*(Isn't this what we call wise?)*
*That young love is not love at all.*
*Love needs depth, truly that Voice says,*
*It needs the substance of scars,*
*And so it demands the sacrifice of years.*

*But she felt, in all that excess*
*That is the giveaway bell of youth,*
*That she could not live, not for a moment,*
*Not for another, single, unlivable day,*
*Without him.*
*So you see, it felt to her, true or not,*

That young love was all she would ever have.
And when she died,
At the unknown hands of someone who had
Taken the slow trouble to know her,
Walk her routes, a seeing-eye shadow
Trailing her home like the eye of a storm,
Love had been forced from her,
Adult and unreasonable and ending in
A bloody, trampled, desecrated mess.

So it stands to be said,
In a voice that is not wise, not distant, not always right:
Let people love where they will.
Let them love when they will,
And with whom they will.
The substance of scars is the way of inescapable strife,
And years can belie what ought be the way of life.

There. A vague reference to the murders over inter-caste marriages that had been in the news lately, disguised in enough metaphor to make it look artfully esoteric, starring a tragically raped-and-killed kid. Some rhyming to show ability, some blank verse to make it look progressive. Enough to make it look like I had made an effort.

———

The number I had saved on a dark, cracked pavement with fingers that were trying not to shake flashed on the colour screen. Holy shit, he was here.

'Hello?'

'Come down.'

'Are you here?'

'Yup.'

I slid into the seat beside his, thinking only that I was sliding into a seat beside Kage.

We drove around the block and parked in a narrow alley. He popped in a CD and the player slurped it up.

'Ready?'

'Very.'

*Of implication, insinuation and ill will, 'til you cannot lie still*

'That was amazing.'

'It's their best one yet.'

'What's it called?'

'Carnival of Rust.'

'Nice. Can we listen to it again?'

And we did, several times. Moved on to the rest of the album, listened to it for a couple of hours.

Eventually, I had to say, 'Hey, so I lied at home about going for a tuition class, but there's no way anyone's going to buy that I've been sitting through it for over two hours. I should get going.'

'Okay, thanks for listening.'

'Are you kidding me? Totally my pleasure, dude.'

'Oh hey, I forgot—I nicked this for you from the trophy room.'

He lobbed something at me and miraculously, I caught it. 'Shamiana 2008' inscribed on a dull gold medal.

'Did you steal someone else's medal?'

He laughed. 'No, goose, you won. I told the prefect that I
know you and you'd said you wouldn't be able to go to the prize
distribution thing tomorrow.'

That burst of joy, then. It's unavoidable.

'How did you know I'm not going to the prize distribution
tomorrow?'

'You know that girl Sudeshna on your dance team? We used
to be in Kalu's choir together. She called right before I came
over and told me that that Dr Roshan of yours is banning all
of you from returning to St Jude's after those guys were caught
making out in the toilets.'

'I mean, at least go to a secluded classroom or something,
you know?'

He laughed again. 'Yeah.'

I rubbed the medal like a lucky coin. Some of the surface
shimmered on to my fingers.

'Ha, I can't get over this. There must have been students,
or at least very young teachers on the judging panel, because I
didn't even write, like, two hundred words.'

It worked.

'Must have been two hundred really good words, yeah?
Congratulations.' He smiled and drove away.

————

He called me later that night, and we talked till three in the
morning. The next night, till sunlight. This went on for a while.
By the end of a couple of weeks, it had become a delicious

habit. And even as I berated myself against that pathetic superficiality, hating myself for the almost-grateful thought, I found it incredible that Kage, *the* Kage, spent his nights talking to a plain Jane like me.

'Have you heard 'Don't Cry' by Guns N' Roses? I'm obsessed with it.'

I could hear him drumming a beat, probably that song's, on some surface. A table or his headboard or, if he was lying in bed like me, his thigh. I felt very close to him.

'No. Can you play it for me?'

'I could sing it to you.'

Kage was the first boy I talked to, really talked to, said things to, asked and was asked questions by. I memorized the responses that shaped him in my mind. It was the first time I had impatiently waited for my parents to go to bed so that I could crawl under the covers with my phone. It felt like levitating, like taking driving lessons in a Lamborghini.

---

'Hey. Can you talk for a minute?'

'Sure, what's up? You sound excited.'

'I am!' And he laughed.

I settled into my sheets, excitedly waiting to be the person he would expel his excitement to.

'So you know that girl Sudeshna I told you I was in choir with? I just kissed her.'

The big smile in his beautiful voice crushed me a little.

'Really?'

'Yeah. Tara, man. I've liked her all these years—it's crazy.'

I felt so young. Like I didn't know anything at all.

'Oh that's so great, Kage!' Too bright, tone it down, ask something. 'Did you actually have the sense to ask her out properly or did you just float away after making out?'

He laughed. Don't laugh. 'Damn, you got me. I'll ask her out tomorrow. What should I say?'

Anger surged. Not at him, only a little at myself. Mostly at a system where the sexes have virtually no avenue to mingle before they're drunk on the cocktail of being teenagers. It makes us do stupid shit like this, leaves us unable to recognize things for what they are, lets us out with all the naiveté of a fresh heart into a world just waiting to bump it around like so much rubble.

So I sat there, settled into my sheets, clutching my new phone to my hot ear, working out the best strategy for him to ask Sudeshna out. And after it was over, in all the excess that is the giveaway bell of youth, I fell back on to the pillows like a bloody, trampled, desecrated mess.

———

I keep trying to remember how hot it was, but those days of school have a brushed tint of cold blue inextricable on them. This is odd, because I know that it was almost always very, very hot. Stewing, we would sit in class soaking our school uniforms into transparency and hues of ink, under fat old whirring fans that were as ineffective as they were noisy. Button and I carried hand towels in our pockets to mop at our sweating eyeballs, and often used them to cover our faces and fake coughing fits over parodies in the Bitching Book.

But why can't I remember how hot it was? Why does the scene that I replicate in my mind fail me by insisting that the memory I know to be true is a lie?

———

Many years later, during the time that marked the social media pandemic, I saw a picture of Kage with the girl he had married. He'd lost a lot of weight, chiselled out, become an artist famous amongst those who didn't like famous artists. She looked like a sculpture made of milk and china, elfin and fragile, just about the loveliest girl you ever saw.

# April

9810000001981000000198100000019810000001

'Mr D!'

'Hey, you! How are you?'

'Heartbroken and confused. You?'

'Nowhere near as excitingly fraught as you, it seems. What's going on?'

It was part nervous babbling, part uncontrollable need to filter my feelings through his perspective (they came out looking very different on the other side). I found myself telling him about Kage, the fest and the medal and the songs and everything I'd foolishly thought they meant.

I could hear him laughing midway through it, so I tried to wrap it up briskly, like a grown-up.

'So yeah, just, you know, the heartbreak of first love and all that. I'm such a goddamn cliché. Terrible, isn't it?'

'Not nearly as terrible as affecting a blasé pretentiousness, kid. Don't do that.'

I shrugged at no one. 'It hurt. What else am I supposed to do.'

He let out a last chuckle. 'There, there, come now. I'm

sorry for teasing. But that wasn't love. That was a first crush. Sometimes the two are hard to distinguish from each other. Know this—when you do fall in love, it will blow your bones hollow.'

Sharp bumps prickled at my arms and legs. 'Have you ever been in love?'

'The great thing about first crushes, though, is that they prime you with torrents of inspiration. Let's have a gander at the brutalized poetry, shall we?'

'What? No! I didn't write any brutalized poetry. What kind of sap do you take me for?'

'Don't you lie to me.'

I wasn't, not exactly. I'd written plenty of brutalized poetry, but none of it had been about Kage.

'Fine, fine. I—do you want me to send you one?'

'Mm, why don't you read it out to me?'

Caught between an intense shyness and not wanting to appear churlish, I jumped into the water.

'Okay.'

'Thank you.'

'Should I start?'

'Please.'

'So when he does leave,
a deliberate movement he isn't aware of,
a part of me will break
into pieces; shiny, torn
different, varied
a rainbow of tears and screaming
agonizing never leaving

scars brutal and red and sprinkled with blue
I think they are what they seem
taken from me
forced from the loss of Safe.
I am not safe
and it's all within me;
locked away, unexpressed,
except here, on this page
would there were bloodstains
strong enough to be strong enough.'

Splash.

'Hm. You, like me, have the very bad habit of flirting with cliché.'

I sank.

'The good news is that you have amazing words, and a pure connection to the emotions they come from. You end up defeating the dozen clichés in this because of honesty, which is always a defence against cliché.'

'But?'

'No buts. You just need breath. And lose the last two lines.'

'Breath?'

'Spaces between the words, to let them breathe. I'm sure there's some professional terminology for it—I just call it breath. Hold on, I was taking notes—give me one second. Okay, here, try writing it like this:

'So—when he does leave,
deliberate movement unaware,
A part of me will break
Pieces, glisten, torn.

So, so, many
pains
different,
varied
rainbow of tears
screaming—
agonizing never leaving.

Scars brutal and red
sprinkled with blue
they are what they seem
taken from me,
forced—the loss of Safe.

You left me,
and it's all within
locked away, unexpressed,
except here, here
on this page.'

I felt a rush of distinctly unfamiliar form and substance, pulsing to know the taste of his lips and the feel of his skin, everything like an ache for equilibrium.

'Tara?'

The only note of shy hesitancy I'd ever heard from him. It fuelled the hunger, the desire—whatever it was; a want transformed by its fierceness into a need.

I struggled to cover up the lust lodged in my throat; my voice came out unnaturally high. 'Oh. Oh that sounds a lot better.'

'Mmhm.' He'd settled back into himself.

'You're a really good writer.'

'This was actually editing, not writing.'

'Well then, you're a really good editor.'

'True.'

'Also exceedingly modest.'

He laughed.

'Have you always been this arrogant?' I was surprised at my own words, at the unexpected boldness that took to me to take liberties.

'Yes. But that's not a bad thing.'

'I know many who would disagree. I'm not half as bad as you, but I still get the whole "she has way too much attitude" line at every damn PTA meeting.'

'Oh. See, the thing about arrogance is that you need to back it up with enough substance to justify it. Real achievement, and knowledge. And a veneer of polite deference to all elders, superiors, what have you. Then they can't say anything about you. They just appreciate not being victims to your fault-finding.'

'Tall order.'

'Not really. Just be the smartest, most engaging person in the room.'

'Yeah, right.'

'What? You totally have the chops for it. You're completely crazy, which is the first and biggest prerequisite.'

I didn't know about that. 'Well, it's easier for some than others.'

'Oh no, I worked very, very hard to earn my right to arrogance. I had to.'

He was a Dhillon; why did he have to? 'Why?'

His voice held every evidence of shrugging at no one. 'I was fat and geeky. I needed something. Knowledge, confidence, all that. And the words to parlay them to great effect.' He paused. 'The words were the most important part, I think. They became my calling card.'

'They still are.'

'Yours too.'

Blood rushed about; I changed to a lighter tack. 'So you trained yourself into an articulate awesomeness, and then what? Sexy chicas all around the world?'

'Ha, yes, for a while. Unfortunately, I have a rather strong tendency towards falling in love, so that didn't last for very long.'

'What kind of person do you fall for?'

'Crazy. Beautiful and crazy.' He sighed. 'Like April.'

'The month?'

'My girlfriend.'

All my boldness proved a fickle friend. I didn't want to know. But I knew I had to ask.

'Why the sigh, Mr D?'

'I wouldn't want to bore you with the frustrating pitfalls of my life, dear girl.'

'I would really like to be bored with the frustrating pitfalls of your life, dear sir.'

He sighed again. Lost, for a moment. 'It was magic when we met, you know. That's hard to shake off.'

'When did you meet?'

'At Princeton. We met, we clicked, we kissed. Magic.'

'And now?'

'Reality's set in. There are problems at the social and lifestyle levels. Her family has yet to take to the colour of my skin.

I have to be in India in the long run, and that's a plunge she can't seem to bring herself to take. Things like that.'

'But—but these are easily circumvented, right? They're just the superficial things!'

'They are, but I'm learning not to underestimate the power of logistics. They matter a lot. Besides, she seems to be falling apart, and that doesn't help matters. Imagine, every single day of your life, pushing up someone who always seems to be falling, no matter the lengths you drive yourself to for them. I've been trying, every day, for the last eight months, to bring her back to herself. Convincing, convincing, praying, pushing, raising her from the dead, taking hits to my own life that I'm not sure I can sustain. It's exhausting.'

'Do you love a memory?'

'Yes. I've thought about that. But then, every once in a while, I'll see glimpses of the girl I fell in love with, and everything comes rushing back.'

'You're bound to her.'

'I'm bound to her.'

'Oh, Mr D—'

'The thing is, I just cannot seem to be enough for her.'

How could someone like him not be enough for anyone? And what a horrible feeling, to feel reduced, to go unrecognized.

If no one hears the tree falling in the woods, don't you lose your mind wondering whether it really made a sound?

'That's awful. That's really just so awful—' I was horrified to hear my voice crack.

'Hey! What's wrong?'

'I—I don't know. It's like the things people feel seep into me.'

He laughed and I could have cried. I could just have cried for wanting to hear him laugh like that again. 'Why are you so much like me, you crazy little fool?'

My voice came out very small. 'Isn't that a good thing? You're awesome.'

'Not necessarily in ways I'd wish for you.'

I sniffed. 'What would you wish for me?'

'Peace, to begin with. Sanity, if the gods feel like being kind.'

I was a teenager, of course. 'Peace is overrated.'

'No. It is not.'

'I would rather be happy.'

'When's the last time you were happy?'

'I'm happy right now.'

'Are you at peace?'

Me and my shaking hands could only laugh, circumventing themselves around the words that could not be said.

'We are not happy unless we are crying. That is our curse and our gift.'

'Jay?'

'Yes?'

'Does it hurt very much?'

'Not quite enough, dear girl. Just a little short of enough.'

I knew what he meant. It was as true of me as him; our happiness came laced with a measure of pain. It validated the feeling. It made us who we are.

I went to bed feeling a heavy weightlessness, oddly empty and full at the same time. Perhaps it was just my bones blowing hollow.

# Freshman

'Tara, Nicole. Nicole, Tara.'

The summer before I left India was a flurry of lunches and dinners and coffees with all those acquaintances one is surprised to have accumulated over barely the fourth of a lifetime, and crinkle-nosed confusion about items on the list of things the university recommended incoming freshmen bring to the dorms with them. Why did I need a pizza cutter? Did pizza in America come as a whole, undivided round pie? And what was a chip clip? All the clips in the malls and markets I scoured seemed firmly designed for sweeps of hair and unruly bangs; when I experimentally tried snapping one around a deep-fried crisp, the entire thing just crumbled to pieces—what was the point in that, exactly?

I addressed all these queries and misgivings to an amused (inordinately, I thought) Hannah. Her comments densely populated the Facebook pages of the university I was going to attend, and she seemed to know what was what. Upon discovering that we were living one floor away from each other, it was immediately decided that, come September, my first order of business after settling into my dorm room would be to go find

her. Now, she pointed to a girl unpacking a pile of boxes on the
other side of the room, and introduced me to her roommate.

I have to admit that it took me a few seconds to recover my
ability to form words the first time I saw Nicole. She has the
kind of deliberate features (small nose, generous mouth, eyes
of an indeterminate hue) and artless grace that combine to
stamp sex and beauty all over any body. Natalie Portman with
Angelina Jolie's swag, a Botticelli in black jeans.

'Holy shit! You're stunning!' Fuck. Why did I just say that?
These people are going to think I'm a creepy lesbian.

'Sorry, that sounded like a creepy lesbian.' My concern
jumped to the possible political incorrectness of what I had just
said. Would it seem like I was insinuating that lesbians were
inherently creepy? Fuck fuck fuck fuck.

Nicole giggled. 'You're fine. I'm bisexual anyway. I can tell
when I'm being hit on, and this isn't it.' She smiled at me again
and I immediately felt comfortable. That was another thing
about Nicole—her unmasked like or dislike for people shone
through in her every interaction. And I could tell that she had
taken an instant liking to me.

'Oh, you're bisexual? Like, both girls and boys?' I was trying
very hard to be nonchalant, attempting to pretend this wasn't
shocking me at all.

'Mmhm.' I thought I felt her acknowledge my nervousness.
Months later, I asked her about it. She told me that she
appreciated any attempt at making her feel less like a social leper
than she already did. In turn, she didn't quiz me incessantly
about growing up in India ('with servants?') like everyone else,
effectively making me feel more at home than the effusive
protestations of those who seemed to feel the irrepressible

need to proclaim wild excitement about naan and yoga when introduced to me.

Her speech had a slow cadence to it, but it was unhesitating, her words perfectly formed. She didn't end her sentences with an unsure shrug or 'you know what I mean' the way I, and most other people of our age, did.

We were interrupted by Ziggy, from down the hall. Room 704.

'Hey guys, I just got some dro in. Wanna smoke?'

Nicole stared at him.

'Yeah no, I don't do drugs. My mom's a cocaine addict.'

Woah. I peered at her, trying to keep my face free of expression. It was a challenge. Did these crazy Americans just say whatever was on their minds? Was this just how people talked here? Should I just blurt out the fact that I'm afraid I've inherited the trait for manic depressiveness from my grand-aunt or that I sometimes spend the whole night pressing drops of blood on to squares of toilet paper, creating a thick pile of little Japanese flags by morning? I decided to wait and continued to listen as she talked about being the mother in her relationship with her mom, and how she had seen shots of cocaine transform the vibrant young woman of her childhood memories into a shaking tremble of a woman. They had taken her for yet another jab at rehab the day Nicole left for college, and the last thing she saw of home was the door of her grandmother's van closing on her mother, waving goodbye to her in a bright yellow sundress.

No one said anything. Sticks of awkwardness were beating a drum of silence. Ta da dum, ta da dum.

'Oh no! Um, so was that hard on you? Growing up and stuff, I mean, you know . . .' I trailed off, feeling stupid. Why didn't one of the others say something? Ziggy had stayed around, obviously. No guy ever left the room voluntarily when Nicole was in it. I resented their silence, because I was new and didn't know how to respond to it. The worst secret I'd heard so publicly divulged in India was a classmate saying she had menstrual cramps. And even then, some of the stick-up-their-asses products of my convent school had tittered disapprovingly at that oh-so-shocking admission. Still, I was intrigued. I wanted to hear more, to find out as much as possible about this beautiful crack baby.

————

3.18 in the afternoon, and the world had been pitched into darkness. The rain drummed a disheartening drone and, struggling through a sodden campus to class, I wondered again why these crazy Americans insisted on functioning normally during such bad weather. Where I come from—that bribed, lazy, communism-stained state of West Bengal—a drop of rain or a squabble amongst political nobodies is enough reason for everything to come to a standstill.

Growing up, 'rainy days' were some of the best ones. The parents who insisted on sending their wards to school through the rain found them either returned home in soaking uniforms and puddling black Mary Janes, or prancing about in empty classrooms under the watchful eye of temporarily benevolent teachers. On one particularly bad rainy day, a teacher decided to take me home rather than let me wait alone for a car to be dispatched and for it to then wade its way through the river-streets at a glacial pace; barely a dozen people had made it to school that day and I lived on her way home. Willing myself to rise above the shackles of privileged thought, I tried to enjoy my first time on a public bus. A few minutes into the ride, I felt something hot and sticky slide out from between my legs, and an ancient instinct told me to press my mouth and thighs tightly shut. The rain had washed everyone on that bus clean, putting us all on even ground for once. But I knew that the shaggy-haired men jostling too hard against the bodies around them were somehow dangerous, that they seemed angry when they looked at me and my teacher, and that I had to keep whatever was happening to me a secret. When I got home to a worried mother, a maid discovered the red stain on my white uniform and, smiling, gave me some rot about finally turning into a woman.

——

On my first night alone in America, I stood at a window overlooking the somewhat familiar San Francisco Bay area, listening to the amazing vacuum of sound that is a padded American suburb. I would head to the Midwest the next day, to God knows what. I had never been to Ohio. Who goes to Ohio? It was the middle of nowhere.

I missed the frantic sounds of Calcutta every day I spent away from home, and took healing trips to Chicago and New York City, where I would sit for hours on the dais in the centre of Times Square and let the sounds of the city soak into me like a thick, therapeutic ointment.

——

I spent a large part of my freshman year sitting with Nicole
on her bed till daybreak, just talking and discovering her at
times, myself at others. We would watch movies that fucked
with our minds and I would go to bed hoping (sort of) not to
have dreams about twisting tongues with Hannibal Lecter. She
protected me, and in return, I loved her. Nicole sprung from
the darkest well I could think of, but she lived under glowing
strings of Christmas lights all year round.

————

Perched on my share of Nicole and Hannah's dorm room (I
spent so much time in there that they allotted a chair to me as
my 10 per cent share), I calculated how many hours of sleep I
was likely to get that night.

About four. Quite good, considering I usually got only
about forty-five minutes, creaking into bed an hour before
my first class began at seven. Classes next day didn't begin
until ten thirty. Happy, or at least content, I interrupted the
short silence borne of a ten-minute study break (that is, a
break from hanging out to study) to ask them what we were
doing that weekend.

Nicole scowled. But she scowled a lot, so I wasn't particularly
concerned.

'Well, I have to start cleaning this room. It's disgusting in
here.'

Wariness reared up inside me. This was growing into a
familiar and uncomfortable situation.

Hannah tensed up, and I could tell she was forcing herself
to relax and control the vitriolic temper that lashed out at

unseeming provocation—that had burnt a cigarette hole in Ashley's stockings last week at a party. When she spoke, her voice was rent with something. Something transparent and heartbreaking and repulsive, an amalgamation of hope and anger and stiff nonchalance.

'Yeah, this carpet sheds like crazy.'

We all knew it wasn't the carpet's turds Nicole was talking about. Hannah was a large girl, with dreadlocked hair that couldn't be washed as regularly as it should have been. I was unwillingly privy to faux-concerned debates on whether it was her personal-hygiene habits or just that her body got away from her, its crevasses too numerous and too deep to clean, but the fact was that Hannah smelled really bad. *Really* bad.

It's astonishing and disgusting how much space this occupies in my freshman-year memories. But then, Hannah was so relentlessly persecuted, with so much venom, by most of those we lived with, that it was inescapable—a daily train wreck I passed on my way to class. Maybe the real fact of it was that nothing helps people feel like they belong as much as ostracizing someone together. Towards the end of the year, she came down to my room on the eighth floor. Pulling me out into the hallway, she grabbed my arm and I noticed, with a feeling of whole potatoes bouncing around inside me, that she was crying.

'Tara, why does everyone keep talking about how I—how I smell?'

I tried to deny it, but stopped midway. She knew; I could tell by how close to breaking she seemed. So I didn't say anything, unwilling to insult her with lies or sear her with the truth.

'Is it true, Tara? I don't really smell bad, do I? Just tell me, please.'

I lunged at the small motion towards the untormenting ignorance she had made.

'Hannah, I don't think so. Listen, it's just Tits and her stupid friends. Why even give a shit about them?'

I was quick to blame Tits, a beautiful, blonde ex-cheerleader who went to great lengths to embody every stereotype in place about her appearance. She had come up to me as I walked past her room the previous evening and, bubbling over with excitement, exclaimed that she had just got her hands on 'Britney's new CD!' I'd stared at her blankly, not even registering until hours later that she had expected me to be thrilled.

But there was something about her that spoke of a hidden intelligence, some mean brightness in her eyes. I had heard her talking to Anna Marie, a smaller, shinier version of her, over the sound of running water in the girls' bathroom.

'I think Kevin's not talking to me.'

'Oh my God, really? Why?'

'I don't even know. He's been weird since, like, last night.'

'Why, what did you guys do last night?'

'Nothing! He had Calc homework to turn in, so I helped him with it, and then we went to bed. That's it—that's all we did. And now he's being totally weird and, and, like, just not being *him*, you know?'

'You helped him with his homework?'

'Yeah. We covered that stuff in AP Calc senior year.'

'Did you tell him that?'

'I don't know, maybe?'

'Tits, you can't let a boy think you're smarter than him. It confuses them.'

'Really?'

'Totally.'

Perched on a toilet inside the last stall, I grimaced at the stench of their ideas and waited until they left to come out.

Hannah relaxed and smiled at me, obviously relieved. The blonde cheerleader was the socially birthed enemy of the mathlete from North Carolina. Tits laughing at her wasn't any sort of betrayal for Hannah; it was only to be expected and disdained with a requisite snicker about stupidpretty girls. I pushed away the image of Nicole spraying the sleeping mound of her body with Febreze, while an onlooking crowd laughed quietly. Then I squeezed her arm, smiled and asked her where she wanted to get dinner.

'Panera. So it's just Tits, then?'

I nodded. She had to have known that her roommate and friends were in on the slanderfest too, but I'm pretty sure that she wanted to believe my lie as much as I wanted her to.

Now Nicole harrumphed and threw aside *The Criminal Mind*. I knew that while the others bayed for social roadkill, Nicole was genuinely affected by the situation. After all, she was the one who had to live with Hannah, the room pungent with BO and resentment. Her aggravation manifested itself in frequent gloomy spurts, and this was one of them.

She left her bed and, crouching on the floor, began to pick up all the pieces of broken hair on the carpet—pointedly at first, and then, as Hannah ignored her completely, in silent, bubbling rage. Looking at her, all I could do was marvel at how easily she grubbed about on the floor, not seeming to care that her hands were touching the dirty carpet. In that moment, I wanted to weep for Hannah, for the fat, unpretty girl who was constantly surrounded by Nicole's glorious beauty, a beauty so brilliant that it didn't even need preservation to shine.

———

Sometimes, I have fits of acute awareness. They are hell. In those moments, I am highly, terrifyingly, aware of everything. I feel the thuds in my chest, the air passing into my lungs, the saliva sliding down my throat; I am aware of how finite I am, how fragile the mechanisms keeping me alive are. I wonder whether I am really any more than the sum of these mechanisms. I mean, I feel like I must be—the thoughts I think and the things I feel are breathed from a higher order. But everything I am can be turned off by one errant second, one stray bus or bullet; I am no more than a replicable machine.

Or am I just an infinite force trapped inside this replicable machine? I hate my body, hate its fragility and its unreliability. Except in the absolute assurance of eventual decay. Occasionally, I start awake and, shaking, stare at my hands, unbearably aware of their existence and their mortality; ashes to ashes, skin to dust.

———

Hannah introduced Asher to us late in the fall of freshman year.

He was the kind of thin that can never get fat, wore a Rubik's cube named Eric around his neck, and was blessed or cursed with the kind of hyperintelligence that comes across as batshit crazy. When everyone in our freshman-year dorm first started getting to know each other, not a lot of people liked him. Of course, the paradigms of pop culture would shift on to his ground in a few months, and that would be that.

A large group of us was walking through my first snow, en route to get dinner at an Indian restaurant twenty minutes away from campus. I was freezing.

We crossed the main campus area and entered the Campus Arts District, which was lined with restaurants serving vast varieties of cuisines. As we walked past an Ethiopian eatery, Asher laughed and said, 'They have food in Ethiopia?'

There was silence for a second before Eki said, 'I'm from Ethiopia, and I'm pretty sure I ate every day while growing up.'

Hannah shook her head. 'That wasn't cool, Asher.'

A couple of people mumbled agreement. I concentrated furiously on not laughing.

I tried once in a while to explain to Hannah or Thomas that he didn't say those things to be mean. It wasn't personal; he just didn't care enough about anyone to consider their feelings at the expense of forgoing a joke.

———

'Tara. Wake up. It's an emergency.'

Something in Button's voice scared me shitless, so I hung up, then called back, thinking only—no, nononono.

'Cookie's dad shot himself.'

I barely passed Biology 101 (and not for lack of trying), so I can't really claim to know what the actual physiological reaction to that kind of paralysing shock is. What I do know is how it felt, how I could feel time slow down and blood rush about. Some of those sayings that appear programmed into our semantic memory suddenly made perfect sense—I now knew what it meant to feel like your heart is about to pound right out of your chest, how it really does seem like your own screaming, hysterical voice is coming from miles away. It all happened in the space of a couple of minutes, but I have relived those moments—of my own volition and otherwise—over countless hours, memorizing them, trying to memorialize him.

'What's wrong?'

Rosa's voice is sleepy, annoyed. Maybe the university had surmised that the conservative Jewish princess and I would steep ourselves in each other's cultures when they decided to make us freshman-year roommates, but the two of us had had problems from day one. She started crying, threw a hairbrush at me and declared that 'in America, people don't turn on the light when other people are sleeping', as I tiptoed around and got dressed for my 7 a.m. class by the tiny bulb on our shared dresser. And I frequently subjected her to Nicole's company as the two of us did homework or talked in my side of the room, watching her flinch every time we cussed or spoke about Nicole's trailer-park childhood.

'I … my best friend's … uncle …' I couldn't achieve any level of coherence. The image of him telling us ghost stories on one of many weekend trips to their country house kept playing in a static-laden, distorted loop in my mind: Cookie, Button and I, curled up in the sprawling living room—comfortably settled into leather, feet dangling on cool, white marble—listening in gleeful trepidation, screaming with terror and delight when the story, told in a low, sonorous voice, ended in a sudden, scary, shouted detail.

And then we would eat. A lot. Crusted cod and thick,

tandoori fries. Lemon tarts and eclairs oozing chocolate-streaked cream. Aunty's special Nutella-filled crêpes, special mostly because they were just so damn good. The ground staff would set up the barbecue and we would grill chicken and sausages and peppers and pineapples. They relaxed then, too; took off their daytime livery and put on an array of florid lungis.

We ate till we had that full, contented feeling that only an excess of very good food could bring us at fifteen. And it gave Uncle a great deal of pleasure. We could tell it did. Feeding people, a house full of stuffed, sleepy kids—these were the things that made Uncle happy. He was that kind of man.

'Well, could you keep it down, please? I still have twenty minutes to sleep before my alarm goes off.'

It was my first taste of the cruelty hidden in the recesses of polite indifference. I had until now been quite unfamiliar with that. There is too little—too little to eat, too little to drink, too little space to think and breathe—for anyone to be indifferent to anything in India. An NRI friend once told me that every time he landed in the country, he felt like he had been packed into a giant sardine tin of people, each person invested in and affected by the next, to an astonishing, unavoidable degree. What had always been refreshing civility in hotels was cruel—quiet and absolute.

There are only a few events in my life that I can transport myself back to with equal clarity, and almost none that I revisit with equal frequency. Sometimes I think tragedy twines itself into our DNA, irrevocably affecting what we become, turning us into who we are.

I count everything in multiples of four. Counting, I know, is the only way to control things. Blink in fours or pairs of fours. Drink sips of four or pairs of four. Aunty Agnes had told me that five is a good number, and so is ten. Never three, and never ever thirteen. Seven has a three but also a four, and eight is two fours or four twos. Twos are half of four—too little. Nine is justifiable, because it breaks into four and five, and four and five are good numbers.

# The First Germany

Tara: Hey there. Busy?

Jay: Nope, you've caught me at the perfect moment.
My flight just got delayed ☺

Tara: Where are you?

Jay: Germany

Tara: Where are you headed to?

Jay: NYC
Is there something going on with you, love? It
feels like something is wrong.

Tara: Why?

Jay: You're asking questions to ask them.

Tara: Well, I wanted to talk to you.
A few days ago . . .

Jay: I'm glad.
And sorry I wasn't there

**Tara:** Don't be silly

**Jay:** Tell me

**Tara:** It was just
My best friend's dad shot himself

**Jay:** Fuck

**Tara:** Yeah.

**Jay:** India? Or America?

**Tara:** Are you asking questions to ask them? ☺

**Jay:** No, I'm cursing the constraints of geography.
Not least because they are currently preventing
me from giving you a hug.

**Tara:** India

**Jay:** Oh, my poor Tara

**Tara:** I really hate being so far away from everyone
I love.

**Jay:** I know.
It hurts.
But stick it out, give it another six months. It'll
get better. And you'll find more people to love.

**Tara:** How do you know, Jay?

**Jay:** I've been through similar roller coasters,
dear girl ☺

**Tara:** What did you do?

**Jay:** Cried a bit, laughed a bit. Drank myself to the doors of death, for a while. Each helps in bits, and not at all at times. The biggest problem was the emotional build-up that refused to come out. It creates a paralysing kind of stasis.

**Tara:** Yes, yes, exactly.

**Jay:** But now you need to start moving again, step by step.

**Tara:** It's just—everything that matters is standing on the thinnest of tightropes. I'm terrified, Jay. I'm too scared to move

**Jay:** Waves of happiness
Touch of pity

**Tara:** What?

**Jay:** You've hit the age—no, the space—where you've started to feel the implications of tragedy, the unsteadiness of the ground beneath our feet. No one ever warns us about how dangerous it is to go excavating for meaning, do they?

**Tara:** So we have no control over anything? No control over ourselves, even?
How terrible.

**Jay:** There is nothing to control, just different parts to find. It is a fallacy to think we're built to exist in some sort of ideal state that we have to knock and pull and push ourselves into. Discovering yourself is a journey, dear girl, not a battle, even though it feels like that a lot of the time.

The important thing is to feel it all. Feel the pain, write about it, acknowledge it. If he meant something to you—and it is obvious that he did—you owe him your pain, and there is no shame in embracing that.

The best way to do it is by writing. I wrote endless letters. And reams of bad poetry. And the words led me out of that paralysis.

**Tara:** What was the last great thing you wrote?

**Jay:** I've only ever written one great thing.

**Tara:** ?

**Jay:** I'm emailing it you.

**Tara:** A letter?

**Jay:** Yes.
Let me know when you're done.

**Tara:** Two minutes

**Jay:** It has now officially been ten.

**Tara:** Done
It's gorgeous, Jay.

**Jay:** Thank you, dear girl.
It's a pity beauty is never borne of peace.

**Tara:** Are you headed to NYC for her?

**Jay:** Where else, who else.

Tara: I hope you're a little bit happier than you sound

Jay: I am. Not by much. But yes, in moments, I am.

Tara: Otherwise, I'm scared for you

Jay: Haha, I'm scared too.
Darling girl, I need to run. They just announced my flight.

Tara: Oh okay! Run, run!

Jay: Please take care of yourself
And email me your phone number so I can call you
Once in a while

Tara: Lol. Have a safe flight ☺

———

I never did send him my number, because he obviously didn't actually want it. But I did start writing—as if I had never stopped, as if putting pen to paper was like riding a bike or swimming. The incidents and experiences and opinions, all flooded my mind at a speed that my fingers raced to keep pace with, some true, many made-up. I wrote one story about an awkward, sordid first kiss—his girlfriend sleeping only a few feet away as he unclasped her neon-green bra—and another about the time a girl sat and picked at a scab on her arm, creating Japanese flags by pressing the circle of blood against squares of toilet paper, her lunatic mind convinced that if she stopped, terrible things would happen.

# Rise Against

'And there's nothing they can do? Even though you have a 3.9?'

'Nope. The lady at Student Services checked to see. There's absolutely nothing they can do to help fund you if you're an out-of-state student.'

It was midway through freshman year and Nicole had done the depressing math.

'So, no, wait, what does this mean?'

'I have to transfer to community college back home in Nebraska, Tara. It's free; there's no way I can afford another year here.'

I was about to ask whether she didn't know that before she decided to come here in the first place, but stopped myself just in time.

Later, after Hannah and Thomas had left the room to get snacks from the vending machines in the lobby, she answered anyway. Slumping down on to her bed, she said, 'I just thought that if I worked really hard and did really well, like I always have, this time things would somehow work out. I figured something's gotta give at some point, you know?'

My jaw was aching. 'It's not fair.'

'Nothing ever is.'

'Did you know that Eki has a full ride here? Her parents are both doctors. Her dad's a neurosurgeon actually, I think.'

'That's affirmative action for you.'

'It's not fair.'

Nicole laughed, like it was funny. 'What is?'

———

Almost five in the morning and we had yet to get any actual studying done.

It was like this every day. We used to stay up all night, in the study room on the Honours floor with its pitted walls and scratchy beige carpeting. The plan was to have a study party and get all our work done—yes, all of it. I would take the stairs up to the ninth floor, armed with multiple readings and essays and take-home homework sheets, and then we would order some pizza, because, well, dinner had been hours ago, and aren't you guys hungry?

Occasionally, we were joined by Tits and her friends, but usually it was just us nerds—me, Nicole, Hannah, Eki, Darya (wearing her Russian roots on her face and clothes), Emily, Ward and Thomas, the cute little token gay boy.

Nicole had a crush on Darya, who was flattered but straight.

After seven hours of pizza and funny YouTube videos and Facebook chatting with the person sitting opposite us, we would head down to the vending machines in the lobby to get cookies and Cokes, and then it was five and we were screwed.

We moved around in packs, donning companions like protective cloaks. One day, classes were called off on account of twelve inches of snow. We went out on to the white, empty streets and had a snowball fight, then stole a bunch of trays from the cafeteria and used them as mini-sleds to slide along the frozen surface of Glass Lake.

———

Nicole enjoyed the idea of Jay. 'It's like one of those wonderful, doomed love stories.'

'I mean, I hope it's not doomed.'

'Well, do you ever see it happening?'

'Not really.'

'Why not?'

'He's a proper grown-up with a girlfriend, living somewhere in Europe, last I heard. And I'm a college freshman who barely knows him. I'd say the chances look slim.'

'You never know what can change over time. Plus, you could always just send out some frequencies.'

'I don't know that I ascribe to your concept of frequencies, to be honest.'

'You will.'

'Right. Anyway, he's also too rich.'

'You're rich.'

'Not his kind of rich.'

I wondered again at how she lacked a reactionary bone in her body—being only inquisitive where she could have expressed a reflexive disgust—and tried to satiate her curiosity by explaining the social structure of money, which, honestly, I didn't entirely understand myself.

'We go to the same places and wear the same clothes, but we're not the same. He's in a different league of money.'

'And that's really important?'

I shrugged. 'I don't know.'

She didn't push further. Unlike Button and Cookie, Nicole asserted her affection quietly, somehow weaving together what I presumed were the opposing forces of personal space and support.

'Hannah wants me to take down the Christmas lights.'

'Why? They look so pretty!'

She shrugged. 'She didn't say. '

'Are you going to do it?'

'I guess.'

'When?'

'Now.'

'Fine, c'mon, I'll do the ones near the dressers and you take the other end.'

'Thanks, you.'

'Don't be stupid.'

I watched her loop out a string of lights entwined around the iron stead at the foot of her bed and copying the motion, looped lights off dresser handles and wardrobe curtain-rods. They went back to being plain wood and plain steel. Just wood, just steel. No light.

We worked without talking for a while. It made me very happy that we could.

'Hey, do you want to go to the We the Living concert tomorrow?'

I turned around to see that she was sitting on her bed, wrapping the loose strings of lights up her arms and legs.

'Jesus, what're you doing? You're going to burn yourself!'

Nicole smiled her slow, big, brilliant smile. 'Oh come on, Tara. *Lighten* up.'

I started laughing. 'You're batshit crazy, you know that, right?' She laughed too. 'C'mere.'

I went over and slid into bed with her.

Beds are personal; they are spaces for one. Sometimes for a plus-one. Generally, in those freshman dorm rooms with gathering groups and restricted seating, the unspoken norm was to sit gingerly on the edge of someone's bed when alternative options ran out. Legs swung against soft comforters, denim brushed duvets in pinks and blues and reds. But I sat deep on Nicole's bed, all the way along the breadth. Rested my back against the wall, against the pillows she slept on. Kicked my shoes off, rubbed damp socks on a bright green spread.

As she sometimes did, Nicole scooted closer and wrapped herself into me. She sidled on to my lap, settled her tiny body along the ungainly bumps and contours of mine. I felt a warm back down my front, arms and legs beaded with little glows of light twined around mine. There is a fairy on my jeans. Fairies on brown skin and black fleece.

She is so, so beautiful. Buttery, cool expanse of skin. Soap and something floral, hair trailing honey on my neck, down my chest. And for a minute, I don't quite know what to do with my hands. I don't quite know how to hide the quickening of my pulse. Can she hear my heart? Will she move away?

One of the tiny bulbs on the string of lights burned a round, reddening spot on my arm. I picked it away from my skin, held my breath. She stayed. I breathed.

'I love you, Tara.'

'Would you ever make out with me?'

She laughed a mildly surprised aren't-you-straight?

'Maybe, I don't know. Would you?'

Honey moved left and right on my neck.

Stung, hurt, petulant, and reticent to show it, I asked her why. I tried to sound amused, settled for casual.

She said, 'Because I love you.'

'So?'

'You're the only relationship of value I've had outside of my mom—and you know how that works out—that's not sexual in nature. And it means a lot to me that I can have that.'

I didn't say anything.

'You're the best friend I've ever had, Tara.'

It felt like a request, so I nodded and started asking about plans to go to the We the Living concert.

————

Sometimes it hit me—where I was, what I was doing, who I was with.

'This is America!' a sudden voice would shout, in me but not mine. 'This is the real America! Real life in America. Think!' And then, less exultant, more pensive, 'Just to think . . .'

These were the unicorns. This was where they lived. They ate chicken salad sandwiches at Potbelly and drank Cherry Coke. And I—*I* ate chicken salad sandwiches at Potbelly and drank Cherry Coke.

The length of distance loses weight as it grows. The miles that are traversed through the air are forgotten as they are left behind. We measure our distances in time and money, in flight durations and ticket prices, in morning-here-night-there and calling-card rates. On planes, we glance at the miles travelled and left to travel (eight three something something, one two something something), but we judge where we are by the glowing little numbers that tell us it's been fourteen hours since Indira Gandhi International. Only two-and-a-half left to go, thank God.

I felt this distance, at these times. I felt the miles and not the hours. The enormity of the space between where I was and where I had been. The physical, tangible reality of it—the sandy stretches striated atop black seas of liquid gold, the twinkling cities that passed by in such quick minutes. That endless, endless blue—above, below. A space so large that, at some point, we cut through a sky that is half day, half night. A space so great, so enormous that it can hold two realities, that it can distort that great, big, solid thing—Time.

When I wasn't busy examining the enormity of realities, other more pressing concerns occupied my mind. Such as the fact that I was still ugly. Shit. I had thought that problem would sort itself out by the time I was ready for college in America. At twelve, I thought that the baby fat would be taken care of by fifteen. At fifteen, I was convinced that I would find a way to tame my box-shaped afro into straight sexiness by eighteen. At eighteen, I was fucked.

The vast array of beautiful blondes, brunettes and everything in between pronounced the contrast between what I was and what I wanted to be. There was effortless American beauty all around me, and I, all pudge and glasses and frizzy hair, sized up the competition and prepared to settle into celibacy.

The heat and filth of India ensure that unless you come from the sort of money that can completely insulate you against them, you always carry around the sheen of poverty on your person. Unless every environment you subsist in is completely air-conditioned, you're probably going to be spending a good nine months of the year wallowing in and smelling like a pool of your own sweat. The hideous pair of tennis shoes I wore in the infancy of my affair with America served as an endless source of fascination for me during those first few months. I would gaze at the soles of the shoes, repeatedly amazed that they looked so very clean—unsoiled, really—despite my having traversed up and down campus and the nearby roads in them. Back home, the streets would have deposited enough dirt and mud to strip the newness off any footwear in a single outing.

But even money can't buy effortlessness, cannot guarantee the kind of innate confidence that comes of being born into the gamine, fair-skinned global ideal of beauty. Sure, the PYTs combing the shops in the newly built malls and plazas in New Delhi can spray on all the Givenchy and plaster themselves with all the make-up that they want, but there is no achieving that enchanting scent of cleanliness and soap, that clear-skinned radiance that seems to belong exclusively to American girls. I remember a professor in London joking, as we gathered for a group photograph on the final day of a college study-abroad programme, 'All you Americans with your healthy complexions and beautiful white smiles gather around the front while we British hide our sagging skin and rotting teeth in the back.'

We all laughed, but it was true. American girls have a beauty all their own, attractive in a way that even Italian elegance and Parisian charm cannot compete with. There is a palpable joyousness to them, the way they throw their heads back and laugh, showing off an ease of existence in their own skin.

The unicorns shone right in front of me now, within touching distance of my fingertips. I couldn't imitate their looks, but everything else was fair game. Over time, my wardrobe, representative up till then of an Indian aesthetic with a profusion of colours and prints, turned into a smorgasbord of blacks and greys, of layered shirts, and leggings and cardigans embedded with distressed crochet. I invested a small fortune (money *and* time) to tame my hair. In class, I would watch the way the unicorns wrote and imitate the rounded, speculative movements their brightly polished hands made, so different from the scurried note-taking by grade-crazed students in India. I learned how to infuse a sense of purpose into my gait, adopted a near-perfect Midwestern accent, and listened to The Shins.

Sometimes, as I walked around Columbus, I thought about Marilyn Monroe—and how so many of the girls walking around exhibited that buoyant sexiness characteristic of her immortally laughing self, encased for eternity in white and Warhol. Occasionally, at a party or in a city where no one knew me, where my anonymity gave me a floor to reinvent myself in whatever incarnation I chose, I pretended to be from Dayton, Ohio. On those nights, I'd force an ease of manner, animate my eyes and hope to fool everyone in the room. But within the course of a few hours and several beers, all my Indian reticence of movement would be back on field. I'd falter, shake my head no, smile a 'never mind' and long to leave. I don't think anyone else could tell, but I always noticed the moment America slipped away from me.

Maybe American beauty is a religion, a higher calling you need to be born into. Maybe Marilyn is their Mother Goddess. Maybe there is a giggling girl trying—but not too hard—to suppress her playful white dress inside every American woman. And maybe the rest of us can do nothing but stand by, mesmerized and resentful.

———

It was a funny-looking group walking under the bright lights to the Campus Arts District. I wasn't sure what had come over us but on some experimental impulse, Nicole, Hannah, Ward and I had decided to go out to a club.

I got into my tightest, darkest jeans and the only shirt I owned with sequins on it, then helped Hannah struggle into a swathe of black polyblend. Ward pulled himself away from the room where several of the nerdiest boys on campus sat around playing *World of Warcraft* and growing incidental beards. Nicole slipped into a simple green dress that floated over the perfect lines of her perfect body, and I laughed inwardly at the unintentional foil the rest of us were providing for her.

Ward smiled at me. 'Oh hey, Tara, you look so nice.'

I felt a fierce rush of affection for Ward, for his bear-body and sweet eyes and brotherly arm on mine—because I knew he wasn't lying even though what he'd said wasn't true.

We entered the club and I was immediately nervous, borderline terrified. How did Tits and her friends do this every weekend? The dark room was pounding with the reverb from what felt like a thousand speakers beating in sync to the pull and thrust of a thousand bodies. On raised platforms dotting the edges of the throbbing space, bodies were drunk and more naked than not, writhing against doppelgängers and poles. The four of us stood around the entrance, a little confused and very wary.

'I don't want to be here.'

I turned to Hannah and saw how uncomfortable she looked. 'Why don't we go in and get some drinks, Hannah? That seems to be the thing to do.'

Ward agreed enthusiastically and started leading the way.

A hard jostle to the bar and some Lemon Drops later, Ward and I were pleasantly buzzed, looking around with interest rather than terror, taking fascinated anthropological stock. A group of boys were sipping beers by me at the bar and, somewhat scared, I edged away.

Nicole had abstained from drinking and was dancing eye-to-eye, hip-to-hip with some guy, smiling over to where I stood with Ward every now and then. Hannah was watching her and drinking, downing, sloshing full glasses at a rate that told me we'd have to leave soon or risk a very public fit on unfamiliar territory.

I just knew that Hannah would spend the next couple of days in an angry huff, and wondered, again, why it bothered her so much.

Nicole's beauty gave me a perverse sort of pleasure. Demystified something that was very unpleasant as a mystery; not being part of the club didn't feel too bad as long as I had someone on the inside ridiculing everything that went on behind its closed doors.

Unicorn she was, yes, but she was *my* unicorn.

# Boom Forest

Hatch was a hard-assed old motherfucker. He stalked into Creative Writing 201 (Introduction to Poetry Writing) five minutes early on the first day and asked us all to take out a sheet of paper and a pen.

> 'Much have I seen and known; cities of men
> And manners, climates, councils, governments,
> Myself not least, but honour'd of them all'

He paused. And looked around the room with amused eyes and a bald head that disguised his age. It was a clearly calculated beat—but that didn't matter, because it worked. 'Write down the name of the poet who composed those lines. Do not guess.' He played another beat. 'Write it only if you know it.'

I scribbled 'Tennyson' and hoped it would be enough, because I couldn't remember whether his first name was Alfred or Albert.

He waited till there was no more scratching, no more rustling. No more pen-to-paper sounds.

'Those of you that did not put down Tennyson's name (yes!), please leave the room.'

No one moved till he went around to the table in the front and set down his worn brown leather briefcase. He took off his suede-patched tweed coat, folded it and hung it over the back of a chair in the empty first row, then took a seat. Comfortably settled in, he looked around the room, mild inquisition written on his face and fingers, which were tapping the table top.

He wasn't joking. Three people got the message and left.

'The rest of you, arrange your chairs in a circle. Sitting scattered like this is no way to learn about writing.'

Seated in a circle, we waited.

He took his time.

'Concrete imagery. Don't tell me the moon is shining; *show* me the glint of light on broken glass. Anton Chekhov.'

'Painting a picture. Showing, not telling. This is *the* most basic and *the* most indispensable writing tool. And the only thing you will be taught how to do over the next three months.'

I suppose some of us had incredulity spout out of our eyes, at which he barked a laugh and said, 'It will take the best of you that long just to understand what it means.'

———

It's not that Hatch was the most distinguished professor in the English Department, but he was the most respected. Feared, even. One of the course requirements was picking a date on a sign-up sheet to read our poems aloud to the congregation. Four people during every class. The others then critiqued the poem, going around the polite, engaged circle, trying to be constructive. Hatch weighed in at the end, and ripped most people to shreds. The students in question wrote down their commentaries, not looking up, all frantic fingers and flaming cheeks. Once or twice, at the end of class, he asked for a printed copy of one of the poems that were read out. There was surprise, elation and to the umbrage of others—the grand prize.

Hatch had tooled his way to the Pulitzer shortlist a decade ago with his fifth published book of poetry. He had earned that nomination. Learned the craft, honed it. He was a master of the craft and, because of that, we all thought we could learn a lot from him. So we kept our mouths shut, let his tongue run riot and tried not to piss him off.

We reserved this reverence for Hatch, and not for Professor Gershwin, who had yet to hit thirty but was already on track to tenure because his first novel came out to a blaze of glorious reviews, made the Pulitzer shortlist and then won it. Nobody really enjoys being taught by someone who was born with the unfair advantage of prodigious talent. That feels like leftovers, like crumbs and condescension.

———

Nicole and I signed up to read our poems on the same day. Solidarity, support, all that.

We placed our printed sheets in front of us and got ready for the first reader to start. Nicole was uncharacteristically nervous. I could feel the helpless vibrations of her shaking hand, and as I moved mine over to hold it, I saw a note scribbled in her margin: *Everything I hope to never be.*

Our two fellow reciters for the day were Rosie Jones and Andrew Tucker. Rosie was one of those completely inoffensive, utterly nondescript people that are necessary in every story to provide some breathing space. Andrew Tucker looked like an asshole—a good face bearing a smug expression, a perfect body over-highlighted in a thin white T-shirt, and sweatpants slung low on his (undeniably well-formed) posterior.

'Why don't you start us off, Mr Tucker?'

## Joe Works on His College Application

"When I cut off his index finger, the purple was almost black
And the cryogenic lab I worked in—I'll tell you about that
                                  tomorrow—
      had taught me to cut when flesh went beyond purple.
So I cut off his index finger and I slashed at his arm
To wake him up. He would have died if he'd slept."

Pause. Water. Gums smacking each other in places,
                Then he resumed—


"Yellow is so forcefully cheery isn't it?"
Looking around at the walls, laughing, and then the sudden,
                unsurprising turn:
"They think the walls hide it. I saw Dr Swire with my wife—
                they'll take my money,
      they'll take everything I won in the lottery."
Leaning back, "At least they don't know I rigged the elections."
                A wheezy chuckle.

Joe nodded without looking up from his SAT prep book.
The man propped thin against his pillows
On the iron bedstead next to him,
Was as ancient as the mountains he had climbed,
And he would just repeat his stories the next day anyway;
The insurance salesman looking back on unreal years,
Fantastic times.
He looked at the imitation TAG skimming strong sinews
on his tanned wrist;
Another twenty minutes and he would be done for the day.'

I blinked. This tool with six inches of exposed Abercrombie underwear wrote that?

Everyone else seemed to feel the same way. The articulated admiration was surprised, sometimes grudging.

Hatch said that Mr Tucker would be better served if he shifted his focus from poetry to fictional prose.

Rosie was up next.

'The Kiss

Your lips are cold
But when they touch me,
I feel warm,
And my hands get cold.
My heart is beating faster now
And you are . . .'

I stopped listening.

When she was done, Hatch informed her that she was using an ABCA rhyming pattern in the kindest voice we had ever heard from him.

I was reluctant to go third (three is a bad number—I don't, I can't), and nervous about how Sarat Chandra would translate here, in America's cold Midwest, away from his pedestal place in Bengali classrooms. But Hatch pointed at me and I had no choice:

'Aubhagi's Heaven

As the gritty wood of the pyre ensconced another end in flames,
The smoky carriage ascended to heaven.
The Untouchable, Aubhagi, watched from a distance
and prayed for the departing soul.

"I look forward to leaving for Heaven
in a carriage of my own, son.
She was the zamindar's wife, and gold adorns her neck and ears
as she journeys to the Gods. Find a little wood, son,
Give me a carriage that will travel to Heaven."

Aubhagi left when the monsoon rains came.
In her last moments, she thought of the journey to Heaven,
Finally, on her smoky carriage along the road paved with skies—

And her son begged for wood.
"I need wood to cremate my mother, sir"
"Please, sir, I can work till the cost is covered"
"Sir, please let me have some wood."
"Please sir, let me have some wood."

"No."

"No."

"Remove the Untouchable's boy."

On the zamindar's lands, he hacked at a small tree;
Night provided no protection when the guards heard it fall
(If a tree falls in the woods, the guards will hear it fall)
And they beat him with wooden rods, careful not to touch him.

"My mother is dead, Lord, I need a little wood.
She died asking for a smoky carriage to bear her to Heaven, Lord,
I need a little wood. They called her Aubhagi,
Lord, since my father left;
Let her have her dream of death, my Lord,
Let me have some wood."

The zamindar considered the young boy
Begging on his knees, hands folder in either prayer or plea
His rigid body trembling slightly; he seemed too brittle to be.
"You may have sticks and twigs that lie scattered on
the grounds."

The sticks were meagre; they barely covered her body
And the smoke came in wisps
But the furling lines of white
Curled round and round the skies
And he thought he saw Aubhagi in the carriage, on her way.'

The reactions were mixed. Some people repeated the advice Hatch gave Andrew—too detailed, too much like a story, comes off belaboured. Others felt the diplomatic need to appreciate a different culture regardless of merit.

Hatch said, 'That was interesting,' with a giveaway inflection to the last word. Whatever, I wasn't surprised. He was bound to hate it.

Nicole was the last to read. And I think it was fitting—what is a finale if it's not grand?

> 'this chair is blue
> and this bed is bare
> and this floor is cold—
> to my touch
>
> this is a small table
> and this door creaks
> and this sink holds capillaries—
> the breath and the blood.'

Nicole's words were bones. Spare, but dense. Unembellished and honest. Heavy.

I liked what I had written, but after hearing Nicole read her piece out, mine rang untrue. My words circled and weaved and tried too hard to find big truths in little things. Heavy-handed.

As we were packing up, Andrew stopped by my chair to tell me he really liked my story.

'It was a poem.'

'I know. I'm one of those jerks who thought you should try your hand at prose.' He smiled, and okay, he really was very good-looking, so that endorphin rush was not voluntary.

'Um, yeah, maybe.'

'Listen, I think you'd make a really good fiction writer. I know I'd buy your stories.'

He smiled again and left.

From the head of the classroom, Hatch called out, 'Ms Mullick.' Instinctively, I panicked at being addressed directly by an authority figure. 'Kindly bring a copy of that poem to my office.'

---

After Hatch's class, Nicole and I would eat a late lunch at the café on campus, where she worked a part-time job behind the counter. She ate weird combinations of food—clam chowder and peach ice cream, sausages with salad dressing. I got the same thing every time—popcorn chicken with sweet-and-sour sauce and a big, fat slab of chocolate cake.

She slipped on a black apron and a black baseball cap after we ate, squeezed me goodbye and went to work. I walked back to our dorm hall and slept in my room for a bored bit. One day, I decided to take a bus that ran loops around campus instead of walking back. I had been in America a full nine months by then and was beginning to feel confident about attempting public transport by myself.

The bus was delightfully warm, and my routine changed slightly to incorporate it after every popcorn-chicken lunch. A couple of weeks on, I didn't get off at my stop—I stayed on and replaced the bored nap with a two-hour ride.

I didn't know it then, but by staying on the bus that day I would one day find the route to some small salvation.

———

'Nicky, you can't leave me here by myself.'

There. I said it. The day before it had to happen, in desperation, I made that inexcusable, futile, selfish request.

She tried to spread the balm of a lie. 'You're not alone, Tara. You have Hannah and Thomas and Darya. And hey, you and Asher seem really into each other.'

'Don't. You know what this place is like without you.'

And when she hugged me a commiseration, it hurt the most.

The last time I saw Nicole was on the day we moved out of our dorm and went our separate ways as summer strolled in. Intentionally the last two to leave, we hugged a final-feeling goodbye and I watched honey-blonde hair and an orange sundress climb into the back of her grandmother's van.

———

Breathe. Breathe in fours. One, two, three, four. Loop. One, two, three, four. Talk. One, two, three, four.

Four. Always, always fucking four.

# White Noise

Sit, soar, cruise.

The plane smashed through the clouds. They broke. They ripped down their cottony lengths, shredded and scattered, and let us through.

I felt it a folly. I always do. A squirming inside that rings like a warning—my entrails shaking their tails no. It feels wrong to tear our way through the skies. Blankets the air with a sense of the ominous, of portending something terrible—maybe a lesson, maybe an ending—this flouting of gravity, these careless strolls through God's corridors.

We are not as great as we want to be, are we? *Are* we?

We cannot break our way through the skies. We *do*, but cannot—not for long. What happens when the skies have had enough? What will hold us steady in the clouds then?

And feeling mad like a prophet, I could only wait for us to fall through them or crash into something, to crawl, dizzy, out of our seats and look down at no world below, to realize—my GOD, we are skywrecked! A great planeful of people just disappearing into the clouds and never heard from again, lost in the vast empty endlessness of the skies . . .

The boy seated next to me was so beautiful— I was huddled against the window because he was so beautiful, so I wouldn't accidentally touch him! I couldn't quite pinpoint his ethnicity . . . he had my dark hair and my not-white-not-dark skin, but his eyes were pale shots of green. Drinks were brought around and it was a cranberry juice with the R's rolled the American way for him, apple in the same intonation for me.

Do beautiful people know the tremendous possibilities of their lives? Do they know that, at any given point of time, there is the full, distinct possibility that someone is regarding them a revelation? Someone is watching the curves of their bones, feeling the relentless pull of the very way they are arranged.

I felt a terrible longing (because that is all jealousy is, really) to be *this*—this thing we call beauty that lies under everything great that has ever been done. Every great monument, every timeless song, every pimply kid building resolve against the shining head of hair blocking his view of the blackboard— bubbling over with want.

And I did what any body that shares an exhausting relationship with itself (conciliatory, scolding, rationalizing, pleading) must: delved under blankets. Hid. Behind an iPod, behind a BlackBerry. Held up a phone screen and scrolled through a playlist until I found my old friends, the Poets from Finland, who were all that remained of the first boy I ever knew.

A whooshing dip. Sudden, sharp thud.

The world had changed. The world was a roar of hot air.

A year away, and already I had outgrown my home. Calcutta rambled past me like a spatter of embarrassing relatives. I had to avert my eyes from the florid posters peeling the paint off buildings, past the teeming masses of unattractive humanity in bright, cheap polyester.

A few weeks ago, while I was riding a campus bus to an early-morning Eisenstein screening, a patently Bengali man climbed on board, toting a large plastic bag stamped with familiar, curling letters. His eyes had paused at me, hesitant but curious. I had looked away, feeling tainted with a stain that seemed to go deeper than skin, seeping into my emotions, and then, still deeper—right into my core. Wedged between worlds, I was a bridge, blurred at the edges—a person with a personality in perpetual flux.

———

Nothing much had changed at home—other than Polo, who had shot up by several inches, as fourteen-year-old boys are annoyingly apt to. He towered over me now and, concerned about my elder-sibling superiority being challenged, I took a shot at establishing my old position of dominance.

It was past midnight. Everyone except us, including the servants, had gone to bed. Polo was ensconced in the blue beanbag that had taken the shape of his behind over time and thousands of hours of *Grand Theft Auto*.

'Oi, go get me some ice cream.'

'No.'

'Excuse me?'

'No.'

'I told you to go get me some ice cream. You need to go get me some ice cream.'

He lumbered up from the beanbag and walked over. I had to crane my neck to make eye contact.

'What do I need to do again?'

I gulped. 'Nothing! Just kidding!'

Dammit.

I padded back to my bedroom. It looked just as it had on the day I left, like the room was rubbing mortality in my face. I've missed this place, I thought, trying to push away the niggling discomfort of knowing that my writing desk will outlast me. Yes, I have. Even though returning is never easy, I've missed it.

———

I saw a card on the study table, sitting on a small pile of 'Maybe Attending'. I picked it up because it had 'Dhillon' printed on it. Bottom right, set in custom font. It was understated, lovely. I touched the smooth, expensive paper and the seal gave easy way.

It was a wedding invitation.

Was it his wedding invitation?

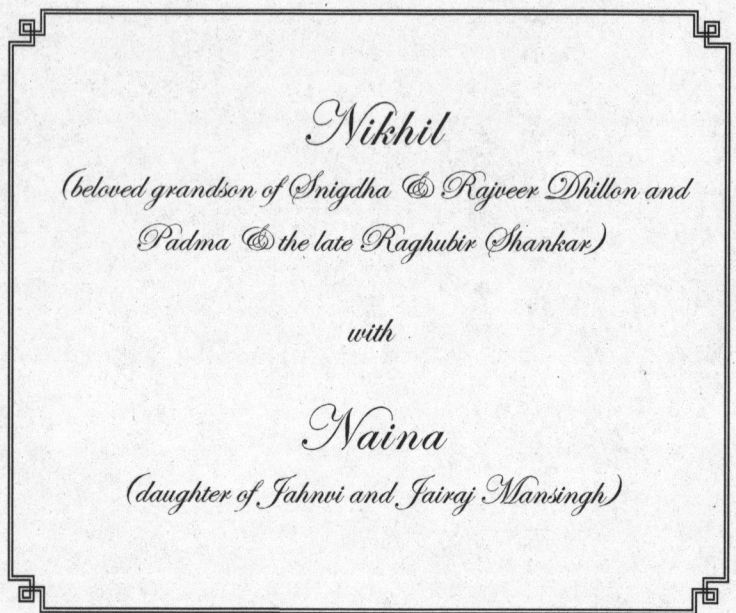

*Nikhil*

*(beloved grandson of Snigdha & Rajveer Dhillon and
Padma & the late Raghubir Shankar)*

*with*

*Naina*

*(daughter of Jahnvi and Jairaj Mansingh)*

I realized that relief had sunk me down on my father's brown leather recliner. The aftershock of horror lingered, mixed a cocktail with the exhausting relief and made me feel drunk, light-headed, dizzy.

Not him. Not Jay.

A month later, I saw him at the wedding—with the girl he loved. Just a glimpse, from a distance. They looked good together. She looked endearingly lost in her sparkly pink lehenga, though it draped beautifully, highlighting the lines of gold in her hair, showing off a thin line of thin waist. I wondered why no one had told him that it was bad luck to wear black to a wedding, and then laughed into my lemonade—because someone probably did.

The two of them were laughing as well, having a personal moment, and I tried not to look—I forced myself not to intrude. I turned and walked away, but not quick enough to miss the expression on his face, not quick enough to miss the adoration in hers.

I wanted to hate her, I really did. But I couldn't help seeing her through his eyes, and it wasn't the crushing drain you'd expect, no. It was merely the dull throb of understanding how it felt to have her lovely hand seeking his arm in reassurance, the small, persistent ache of knowing how it felt to have the stunning blue of her eyes cut so deep that they would be permanently etched into him.

I wanted to hate her, but he looked so happy. And for that, in some small way, I had to love her too.

I had to love her and I had to love him, and it was too much. It was too much.

There would be a room on a street in a house with a window by the bed; I would look out over the Amstel.

There would be a boy in a blue jumper under the watery lions in Piccadilly.

There would be glitter in the blow, the search for a lost song, rain in New York and car windows that turned into mirrors I couldn't look into.

There would be a certain kind of freedom, once in a while, that I always ended up finding I didn't want.

Funny how that works.

## *Mala Di*

Button, Cookie and I were curled up on my bed, all set to talk until light broke through the windows. We were tired out from the adrenaline rush of the past hour, having snuck Button out of her house and into mine for the best-friends-only slumber party.

We'd recruited a reluctant and licence-less Polo to drive me over to her house and catch her as she scaled and jumped over the boundary wall—all while Cookie kept a nervous lookout back at my place. Button gave him a quick, excited hug when we made it home and up the stairs without getting caught, and he broke into the kind of grin usually reserved for greeting his dinner.

It was the happiest I'd been in a long time.

We were all still subdued, of course. I'd even felt hesitant about asking Cookie whether she wanted to come over and spend the night because my parents were both out of town on work. But she had seemed very enthused about the idea, saying yes, definitely, she needed a respite, let's do it, please.

'People, shall we have some drinks?' Cookie pulled out a couple of clear glass bottles from her bag. 'I brought vodka.'

I concentrated on not looking over at Button, knowing she was doing the same.

'Oh. Why?'

'Why not?'

Cookie's voice was entirely level, but I could sense the effort she was putting in to keep it that way. I took my cue and said nothing.

She poured the clear liquid into two more glasses and looked up at us. 'Well?'

We'd always done everything together, hadn't we?

Button picked up a glass. 'Sure, let's have some then.' She winced at the first gulp.

Cookie shook her head. 'Sip it, you ninny. Don't swig it like it's Pepsi!'

'It's disgusting, Cooks!'

'Sip!'

'No! It's vile!'

'You're a wuss!'

I kept taking small sips as Button and Cookie went on in that vein. It really did taste awful.

'Ugh, can we please just put some juice or something in this?'

Cookie insisted that we were absolute wimps, but relented when she saw that we could actually down decent quantities of it if we tempered it with a load of mango juice. I told them about meeting the green-eyed boy on the flight, showed them the Continental Airlines paper napkin with a ten-digit number scribbled boldly in the middle. We laughed and concluded that he was probably just another Asher—flattered but gay. By the time we were halfway through the bottle, Button's head had started lolling about. Cookie nudged her awake, but she stood up, held up a finger like she was about to give a speech, said, 'Alcohol is a waste of perfectly good juice,' and flopped on to my bed, fast asleep within seconds.

Cookie gave me an apologetic look. 'Will you turn her over to her side, Tars? I'm feeling too lazy to get up.'

'Sure, but why?' The vodka seemed to have had the exact opposite effect on me—energizing. Almost like I'd been drinking adrenaline. I liked it a lot.

'So she doesn't throw up in her sleep and choke on her vomit.'

'The fuck?'

'Yeah. Apparently it happens a lot.'

'Cookie, why do you even know this?'

She set her glass down. 'You know why.'

'I know, Cooks, but—'

'You weren't here, Tara. I can't explain it.'

I sat down on the bed, composed entirely of gravity. 'Cooks.'

'I've been drinking with Aditi and Vishal almost every night. It's fun.' She had spoken to me about them on the phone. General things: her college friends, Maggi mates, outstation students from Bangalore.

'Does it help at all?'

She started crying then, and I walked over and hugged her. Did it help, at all?

I woke up early the next morning to clean away traces of the night before my parents came home. I picked up the vodka bottles and made a move to throw them away. But then I stared at Cookie's sleeping form huddled under a muddle of sheets and, terrified by her pain, paralysed at the potential to feel it myself, I couldn't throw the bottles away. I just couldn't. Instead, I stashed it right at the back of my closet and threw an old T-shirt emblazoned with a fading Minnie Mouse over it.

---

I had expected everything in India to stay as I had left it. But Young India was racing ahead, trying to get somewhere as fast as it could. Dropping in to Button and Cookie's colleges, I was amazed to see layered tanks paired with leggings and gladiator flats crowding the streets and hallways. These were the same fashions that I had just seen parading around LaGuardia and Heathrow—but they had already arrived here, riding up on the back of the Internet, glowing alongside the early bloom of social media. I resented it a little. Why did that St Xavier's student look as good in her boyfriend T-shirt—bought at some sweltering stall in Janpath for fifty rupees—as I did in my eighty-dollar thrift-store shirt? What good was my elite status and expensive education if I couldn't distance myself from everybody else?

---

In the morning hours, I woke to the call of a muezzin. There was a mosque near my house, singing out early prayers for the faithful. That song was magic. It got under my skin, trapped itself in my head. And in that moment, I understood

why. What? The spilled and spilling blood, the utterness of
a conviction, not of the body or mind, but the entrancement
borne of a song slicing through vein and tissue to whatever
holds our souls. Of bombs and bursting buildings and not
enough boiling wax to seal it shut. There was no condoning,
nor applause or agreement or desire or dreaming. Just an
understanding of why, of the persuasiveness in spine-tingling,
uncontrollable faith.

But these thoughts were dangerous. I had to keep them to
myself. My thoughts were fine but my skin was brown. And
that is all they would see. They would tell their brothers and
fathers and sisters and mothers and employers and grocers and,
worst of all, their children (because isn't an empty accusation
worst coming from a child? No precedent, no experience to
blame it on, just little deposits of ruin). They would shout out
whispers of alarm and discontentment, entitled and petulant in
the way that only the overfed and undereducated can be. And
I, I would be persecuted (prosecuted?) for feeling the forbidden
Allah bubble through me.

And here, at home, the accusations would be even louder.
No veil of politeness; the lying children of Marx (who have
never heard of Marx) revelled in spectacle and the chance to
feed their hungry masses with publicly executed flesh. Burn
him, beat her, look what we did for you, villager, They were
exploiting you, They are oppressing you, yes They were, yes
They are. Now come, feel the fury and dance with rage. Only
to our tunes, of course. But you don't know that. You never
will. Even as you dance to our melodious lies, even as we use
you to rob Them of their marbled palaces and place them in
our welcoming laps, you will never know that They are all we

want to become.

Does hunger make them blind, these scraggy men with angry eyes, these broken women with hungry lies? Is it only the cold marble beneath my feet that calms my blood, that allows me restful contemplation and hungerless condemnation?

------

The neighbour died in the middle of the night. Silently passed away to a morning of discussions over biscuits dipped in breakfast tea. She was a fairly old woman, left a good address by a good husband, who nonetheless did her the disservice of dying too young.

I wanted to go to her cremation. I wanted to say some sort of goodbye.

It would be silly, though, to ask. They didn't even let me go to my own grandmother's cremation. I think maybe kids aren't allowed in there. Of course, I wasn't a kid any more. But I had been—a kid, sneaking into her bedroom while everyone else waited for the hearse in the hall. Not knowing to *not* be inured to her cold body wrapped in red silk, poking at the space between her nose and lip, which had turned curiously hard. Some of the brown lipstick they'd slicked on her smudged off her mouth while I played with her stopped flesh—and I panicked. I held her hand for a minute, to calm down, then pulled a maid into the room and begged her to fix it.

It's funny to me that kids aren't allowed inside cremation grounds. Funny, and stupid, because hell, it seems like they're the ones most equipped to deal with death and loss. Easily distracted, only temporarily invested; I could have handled so much more as a kid than I can now. When Dida died, I went out to the verandah and pretended to cry because I wanted to be part of the sadness, and someone came and scooped me up and hushed me with a smiley-faced cookie. Now, I somehow saw the dead neighbour's life play out in a sentimental sepia tint. And when I cried for her, because I did, I locked my bedroom door and washed my face before I came out.

The elders of the house—parents and The Wolf and grandaunts—attended her final rites in starched whites. Spotless, clean, bright whites, reserved for funerals and prayers.

I asked my mother if I could go along, and she said, 'Oh no, honey, not at all. You don't have to. Just go ahead with your day as planned and we'll see you in the evening.'

'Well I won't be home for dinner. Going to Blue China with Button and Cookie.'

'Wow, sounds good. I'm jealous!'

'Do you want to come along?'

'No, no, you kids enjoy yourselves. Is Polo going with you?'

'Maybe. I'll ask.'

'Take the new driver, okay? He needs to learn your routes.'

'Cool, see you.'

On the way to pick Button up, I listened to music and mentally debated between Singing Chicken and Schezwan Pork. The radio repeated that song, sung in a dripping, garbled voice, several times a day. *Leggoyah ha, leggoyah hey*. I bopped my head and sang along. It was a good song. An old song. But someone at Power 107.8 FM loved it, played it all the time. This and some cheesy Bon Jovi tune that I wouldn't want to be caught dead listening to by Asher or Jane, but keep secretly stashed on my iPod for Midwestern days when I can only think about the smell of rain-dampened earth cooked by city smoke.

Dinner was delicious. The Schezwan Pork was excellent.

I couldn't sleep that night, so I played that sepia reel in my head again, almost voluntarily. Finally, I scribbled a few silly lines on a piece of my favourite stationery (scratchy handmade paper) and, creaking open his bedroom door, woke up an irate Polo. 'Hey, can you fold this into a plane, please?'

'Wha—?'

'Here, this paper, fold it into a plane na, please.'

'Are you serious?'

'What?'

'Did you seriously just wake me up to make a paper plane for you?'

'Shit, sorry. Sorry!'

'You're a fucking bitch.'

'Please? I'll owe you big time.'

'Here, take it. And get out.'

'Thanks, dude.' I kissed the top of his head and ran out as he roared a disgusted death threat.

I went to the terrace, taking the scary way up, climbing the reel of wrought iron winding around an edge of the five-storeyed house, because the doors along the central tube of landings and stairs had been locked up for the night, their keys hanging from a knot in the trusted housekeeper's sari.

Even the hot summer air cooled down a little, up on the windswept terrace. Feeling like a song by The Shins, I launched the paper plane at the neighbour's dead roof, two storeys below mine. The thick air made a heavy production of it—lobbed it around, eddied it between the buildings, made it dance an elaborate dance in fluid little jerks.

The handmade paper plane landed on a parapet jutting out between the second and third storey. Not my first choice of location, but it would do. It would be part of her house for a while.

> *I knew you a little.*
> *A red telephone on a white lace doily,*
> *Big black glasses (real ones, those),*
> *A mosaic floor, a torn nightdress,*
> *A life lived for someone else.*
> *You gave my brother a chocolate bar once,*
> *A chocolate bar with dried fruit in it.*
> *I was glad he didn't tell you that he didn't like dried fruit,*
> *And I ate it.*
> *I knew you a little, Mala Di,*
> *I wish I had known you more.*

———

That song came on again on the ride back to the airport. I tried to sing along, but I couldn't. *Leggoyah ha*, and there was a lump blocking the way.

Without my voice joining his, the singer's words, in the way that words sometimes do, revealed the shape they were born in.

*Let go your heart / Let go your head*

# Sophomore

We used to go down to the Salvation Army store and buy plates to crash, and colouring books and crayons. In the fluorescent aisles of CVS, Nicole would look in her wallet, look at the tubes of toothpaste she couldn't afford, sigh, and make the impractical decision to save our sanity, to try to be happy.

We would break the plates, drive our voices sore, then go back to her room and colour black-and-white drawings of cakes and lobsters.

I couldn't leave her behind.

I went to our places, to buy our things, to try and do our things.

I threw the chipped blue plate at the dumpster. It crashed a loud, short sound. Too short.

I threw two plates; loud, longer. This was how it had to be done, then. So be it.

I smashed a plate at the gunmetal hulk of the dumpster, then another. I screamed. Smashed. Screamed. Kept screaming, kept smashing. The plates and my voice against that dumpster together, in a smashing, crashing harmony.

I screamed till I had emptied out my lungs, hollowed out one vital organ to try and heal another, and then I was done. Picked up my bag, turtled it on to my back, walked away.

———

There was a pinprick of light reflected on the touchpad of my laptop. I rubbed my eyes, not bothering to remove my glasses. I felt soft, malleable. There was no resistance from my face as my fingers moved across it, and my eyes hurt only momentarily from the pressure I applied to them.

It was 4.37 in the morning. Soon, I would go to sleep, within this hour and the next, and that would be the end of another day. I wasn't doing this right. The days were moving by too fast. I was terrified.

I often thought ahead to the moment I would die, not being able to decide whether I wanted to be prepared or not. I just knew that I didn't want to be gasping for breath. So no drowning, no being smothered by a pillow—nothing asphyxiating of any sort. Can you breathe while burning? If not, then no burning either.

This was a selfish conundrum; I shouldn't care so little about those who love me. Maybe I *was* selfish. That's an awful thing to be. There were so many more terrible things that I'd rather become.

Stop, just stop. Think about the test tomorrow. Think about how hot Asher is and how we almost kissed in the lobby last night. Well, I guess, technically it wasn't night; 4 a.m. is already morning. It would have been my first kiss.

I felt hot. My room was cool, but it was the air-conditioned kind of cool. The air was too still, and I craved a breeze. These were the times I wish I smoked, so I could stop worrying. But I was afraid I would die of lung cancer (probably gasping) if I smoked—that would defeat the purpose of smoking to calm fears of dying, just a tad.

I battled myself all through the second year at college, counting everything, hoarding empty bottles of pop at the back of my closet, convinced that they were the strings holding my world together. It seemed that Nicole leaving so soon after Cookie's father killing himself had snapped a wire, cracked a bolt.

It felt like there was this box in my head, this unopened box that I instinctively knew was best left untouched. That was all I knew about it, though. Nothing else. Was it unstable? Maybe. Would it explode at the slightest provocation? If it did, would the contents that burst forth be kind of bad or very bad?

No idea.

So I was just very careful with it, going to great pains to avoid touching it. And if a gossamer of thought accidentally grazed it—when I was alone and my attention had dropped for a moment and led me back to that old house with Aunty Agnes still in there, talking to her birds, I panicked and stuffed myself full of food and TV and anything else that could distract me the fuck away.

I held myself very still, waiting, waiting, and then I un-arched my toes, let out my held-in breath, moved my fingers. I was in transit, I hoped. Something had to give. Right?

# Junior

Maybe it's Coppola or Wang, maybe it's Passion Pit on vinyl or Jim Sturgess in a speakeasy or just the way time rolls. Nobody knows. But suddenly it was a log cabin in Wisconsin, not a bright boardwalk in California. Florence. Gaga. Rihanna in smoke and leather. Straggly browns and burnished reds, not tints and highlights in blonde. Labels disappeared into linings inside bags and vests, and Chucks in purple and green and tartan and pink spread till plain grey Vans were the new Chucks.

*This is a call to arms to live and love and sleep together.*

There was a change underway. Between high school in 2006 and college in 2009, the tectonic plates under America's feet had been busy shifting the social paradigm around. The hipster was the new king, his feathered girlfriend was queen and Aphrodite. They ruled the campus and they owned the bars. Tits the cheerleader put blue feathers in her ears, Tits the cheerleader wore a leather band around her forehead and a flower in her hair. But Tits the cheerleader. She was Tits the cheerleader. Her dress was too tight, too synthetic. Her make-up too bright, too synthetic. She was glanced at a second too long, a fraction too strong. She did not fit. She should leave this brown bar in the Campus Arts District. She should go downtown and into a shiny, sweaty club. She was not for us. We were not for her two years ago, but she was not for us now.

We listen to Florence now, Tits. Britney Spears is a joke. Unless, of course, you're the pretty little Ashton (denim hot pants and Hello Kitty tank).

Meanwhile, on the north side of campus, near the engineering and mathematical buildings, the bespectacled thickened their frames and tightened their jeans. As high school ended, really and truly ended, their stock rose. And they didn't want Tits either. No, now they wanted the queens and the Aphrodites, and it was about time they had them. It was their due, overdue.

The youth are starting to change.

————

The people who have victory written in their stars, of course, use this gift. They use whatever it is—their luck or their gut, or just their irrefutable genes—to slide neatly into the right slots. Hell, they create their own slots. In their beauty and their brilliance, they are more lethal than Tits and her kind have ever been. They leave us gasping in their wake, widening the gaps, confirming that there will always, always be gaps.

They somehow knew, right after it was real and just before it was too late, to don the plaid, to go to Bonnaroo. They discovered MGMT right before *21* hit theatres. They're in it, they shape it. They're so good at absorbing and understanding that they can do what Tits can't—they can change at will, so that the zeitgeist always forms around them.

It's not that Tits & Co. didn't still carry themselves with the bearings of rulers. They still had mad swag. But they'd lost their kingdom, and I wondered if they knew that. So they built new bars, they got the best jobs. Well, the corporate jobs: Brooks Brothers' ties and Wall Street money. Jobs that sapped the cool right out of them, kicked them into a corner office and out of the zeitgeist. They got away for the weekend with their boyfriends and girlfriends, they took pictures with their parents. Where's that line between growing up and growing old?

I decided that it was time to be one of the chosen ones.

Asher was probably the single smartest person I had ever encountered. He treated classes as a joke, played a game with himself where he saw how fast he could complete exams (that he hadn't flipped open a page to study for). He finished the two-hour exam in twenty minutes. Topped the class. Decried the mediocrity of education with laughs. He dropped his triple majors (finance, economics and automotive engineering) out of boredom and opted for the fluff communications major instead. Decried his obvious self-destructive tendencies and laughed.

It didn't matter. Companies began courting him at the beginning of sophomore year. Start-ups offered him six figures to spearhead their marketing division.

He turned them all down. He took a job as a digital artist for a struggling magazine, worked out of an exposed concrete-walled office in the Campus Arts District. Made less money a month than his second-skin Citizens cost, but that was all okay—as he said, 'It's trendy to be poor.'

It was a ridiculous statement, made at a hungover lunch with him and Jane sitting on one side of a TGIF booth, Thomas and I opposite them.

Thomas laughed at Asher. Directly, straight *at* him.

Jane laughed a laugh that wasn't amused enough to not hold a measure of assent.

I picked Jane's laugh. And moved my shoulders and head in a combination of a shrug and nod.

Are you starting to change?

———

Asher and Jane were both from South Crown. I went home with Asher for Thanksgiving and we drove past the towers of oak ribbing the hill that opened up into those Toyota-lined streets of suburbia. Here, on these streets, in this house, my friend Asher had grown up like a character straight out of some indie movie—with a blind cat, faded clothes from American Apparel and constant existential angst expressed as wry, dry humour. In high school, back when he was still trying to tell himself his fascination with the male form was just anthropological and self-reflective in nature, Asher had been madly in love with Jane. They were friends, but he never had a shot with her because she had always had a steady boyfriend sixth grade onwards. Being one of the chosen ones, it was Jane, and not some blonde cheerleader, who ruled South Crown High School as an irresistible Manic Pixie Dream Girl, even before that was a thing.

After that Thanksgiving, we became quite the tight threesome. I loved that the two of them were crazy and fucked up, and so good-looking and cool that their friendship felt like a prize I had won. To them, I suppose I was both novel and comforting, interesting and only very slightly exotic—never, ever discomfitingly so—because I talked like them and dressed like them and ate like them and thought like them. So I flitted around at their edges, a member by association. Cool enough to be cool, but not on my own.

Thomas tried very hard to ape them, to join in. But he didn't have their intrinsic magnetism, that *je ne sais quoi* which guided them like a godmother. He came from a family of solid, stocky, down-home white folk, indistinguishable from their neighbours or stereotype, while Jane was both adopted and one-fourth Korean and Asher's parents went through just the right amount of silent, civil fighting after their upper-middle-class divorce. Even their bodies seemed to have decided their fate for them: built to be tall and lean, built to carry the fashions of the time, every time. Asher and Jane could never eat themselves into any shape other than the one in power, while Thomas could never morph his body away from a propensity towards the robust, no matter how much he worked out or threw up in the bathroom after meals.

The three of us would pour vodka (the kind that is expensive but comes in cheap, old medicine bottles) into our morning cups of coffee and take it from there. Asher was in the midst of a tumultuous break-up with his first boyfriend. They got into raging fights that sometimes devolved into physical violence. But that mostly just consisted of two skinny boys taking awkward, half-hearted swipes at each other, so it was kind of funny, really.

We used all this as an excuse to fuel our self-indulgence and pretend we were caught in the throes of existential angst, which is, as everyone knows, the best kind of angst there is.

Usually we met at Jack's for underage drinks in between classes. They let us in because Jane was all legs and always wore shorts, even in the winter, when she'd just add a layer of sheer, ripped black tights under the denim cut-offs. We drank our wine through straws so we'd smell less drunk when we returned to campus for our afternoon and evening classes.

At night, sometimes we would get the kind of drunk where we'd run screaming down the streets and into bars, scaring sober strangers and befriending drunk ones. At other times, we would drink a box of Franzia and lie on Asher's bedroom floor in the dark, listening to 'Konstantine' on repeat, talking about how unhappy we were even though we didn't know why, and singing along when our favourite part came on.

'It's to Jimmy Eat World' would send us song-tripping, and we'd follow band after band named in song after song.

And when I was exhausted, when I couldn't casually feel everything anymore, I'd go home to Thomas, which was an easier pretence. He wasn't as smart as Asher and Jane, not as effortless as them. He understood less, cared about the commonplace. And I could keep him at the periphery of my attention as I zoned out to a sandwich and *America's Next Top Model*.

Asher and Jane felt like strobe-lit nights on pure-cut MDMA. Thomas was the slow, comfortable haze of being softly high—marijuana, not acid or Ecstasy. And reality was, well, it wasn't, really. Delving into myself was, of course, never an option. How boring. How scary.

It started because, why not? We were bored. We made brownies. We laughed at everything. It was such a great time, at least for a while. Four giant brownies later, I began to feel distinctly uncomfortable. I could hear the others talking but was finding it harder and harder to follow their train of conversation. Why was I the only one excluded? It had to be because I was different, because I was Indian and not American, like them. It didn't matter how well I thought I merged into life here, didn't matter how comfortable I felt in this country, America would never accept me completely. No, this had to be the weed; I had never felt this way before. I was Thomas's best friend. I knew he liked me more than he did Asher and Jane. Or did I just think that? Everything seemed very clear, but what if this clarity was wrong? What the hell was going on here?

'Thomas. THOMAS. Would you fucking pay attention here for just a second? Tara's been crying like crazy and I can't get her to sto—what the fuuuuuck man, why's she screaming? Tara, stop screaming!'

I threw a ten-dollar antique finish Chinese vase from Target at the wall.

'Tara, just calm down. We had too much and then the milk—it's just that—Asher, what the hell are you doing?'

'I'm going home. Tara's freaking me the fuck out. Move, Thomas, I am not okay, I gotta go.'

'Asher, you can't go home like this! How can you go home like this?' Thomas was starting to panic as well; I could feel it and it made me feel a little better.

'I can't stay here, okay? She's freaking me out!'

'Tara, shut the fuck up, you're freaking us all out! The neighbours are gonna come in here!'

'Good! They need to come and call the cops! Jane, I'm telling you, this can't just be weed! It's been laced with something, I can tell. Like, I think I'm dying—just listen to me!'

'Tara, it's only weed, okay? We just had too much. Just calm down, please.'

Asher left.

From the coffee table, a plastic car smiled at me. I held up the Happy Meal toy. 'Should I hold on to this as my totem pole? Will that help?'

'What?'

'Like in *Inception*. The totem pole. I feel like I'm slipping between worlds—can't hold on to a thought.'

'Yeah, yeah, do that, that'll help.'

Things slowed down. Jane, Thomas and I climbed into bed. We spent the night cuddled up together, panicking at intervals and eventually falling into a fitful sleep. I woke up the next day, still high, and tried to go to class. But I got lost and scared on the way and hid in the basement of the Chemical Engineering building.

———

We met at Jack's early the next evening. I walked in, my mind still unsteady, and saw Asher sitting at a table, sipping wine.

The place was packed, as all bars around campus were. Our school had just won another football game. Yay, or something. To me, the streets and bars looked like the majestic home of some rich, happy cult. Which, in some ways, I suppose it was. Students milled around in college colours, talking excitedly about the football victory last night, like they'd scored the damn goals themselves, like it even mattered.

Asher and I drank our wine in disdain. Never. We would never be part of this cult. We would never walk around declaring affiliations on our clothes, never go to football games and roar investment. We were way too cool for that. We were apathy, jaded irony, Skrillex before the Rolling Stone cover, Florence before *Eat, Pray Love*, and moth-eaten shirts at ninety dollars a pop.

Jane walked in with Darya, and we waved her over.

'Darya, where were you last night? We did brownies. It was horrible!'

'You did? Brownies suck. I did them when I was like, fifteen, with my cousins, and it was seriously like, no, never again.'

'Why, what happened with you?'

'It was like, kind of, I couldn't hold on to a single thought, you know? And so many things were happening. It was fucking scary.'

We came to the conclusion that pot was not for people who already had a lot going through their heads. We were too smart to smoke pot. That was the story.

But I tried it again. And it was better the second time, so I took a bong rip at the next party too. It got fantastic. I could finally reach the sublime truth of The Killers' beats, could finally feel the complete force of *Titus Andronicus*.

It made so much sense to keep lowering myself into the columns of glass-covered smoke, to make it a daily ritual. It kept the nights shorter—which was very important.

Darya reached for the Funyuns and knocked the bong over. The foggy water spilled all over the beige carpet. Thomas laughed. I knew he had to be as high as I felt because sober Thomas would never laugh at a mess he'd have to clean up later.

She squealed. 'Theooo Thomasssss! I'm sorry, do you hate me?'

'Naw, pumpkin, I can never hate you! You're my pet! My little pet! Beepbeepbeepbeep.'

'Oh my God, tamagotchis? I used to love them!'

'Yes! Me too! I still have like twenty of them in the basement back home.'

I had to ask, the question was burning a hole in my throat. Speaking took a lot of effort, though, so it was a while before I said, 'Is it that little thing, with the keychain and the little screen?'

'Yeah, tamagotchis! Did you guys not have them?'

'No, but I met someone who did, once.'

On many weekends, I would eat spaghetti minus the meatballs and watch home videos with Thomas's family. He asked me in an aside whether I was bored. I said, no, watching him as a kid made me laugh. He accepted that answer with a grin and some comment I didn't hear. Thomas and his sister dancing to the Backstreet Boys and screaming down Slip 'N Slides on screen was making my skin rise in little bumps. It's a distorted sort of familiar, a past I lived but didn't live.

I could've told Thomas this. I told him a lot of weird shit. And I knew all his weird shit. But I couldn't bring myself to say it. These longings felt too shameful, too private, to be shared as confessional bonding. I felt like a thief, and these spoils were mine.

----

Thomas and I smoked pot like it was our business. We smoked every day, and every night. Always before we ate. Sometimes while we ate. I inhaled cigarettes before and after class. And it had started with four brownies, and me hiding in the basement.

We lived in a shady part of town, in condo-style apartments where we shared walls on either side with our neighbours. I had to lie to my mother about the kind of area I was living in, but it was all Thomas could afford and I wanted to live with Thomas. At the end of sophomore year, when we were all moving from dorms to apartments around campus, the two people I spent the most time with were Thomas and Asher. Both were fun, semi-alcoholic (in the way that is socially acceptable during college), and gay as the rainbow.

Since I had to pick, I chose Thomas because even though we were close friends—some would say best friends—I never did value him or his friendship the way I did Asher's. So with a foresight I generally don't possess, I moved into 100 Macarrow Street, Apartment D, with Thomas.

I loved the place. It was walking distance to the Campus Arts District, which was, hands down, the best place in the city. There were art galleries housed in crumbling buildings that should have been condemned but instead sold a half-dozen thousand-dollar paintings every weekend, upscale apartment complexes fashioned like Victorian mansions where the spinster professors from the English department lived, quaint little tea shops that cooked meth in the back rooms, and restaurants that served crazy, varied fusions of food—Thai-Barbeque and French-Indian, vegetarian sushi and Tailgate Greek.

Best of all, the CAD was home to the friendly bars frequented by the two communities that were fuelling and forming pop culture: the hipsters and the LGBT, who lived in a cosy, connected world of causal coexistence. That is to say, where the little gay boy went, the pink-haired girl followed, and where the uber-cool, beanie-wearing musician liked to hang on the weekends, the glittering drag queen made her home. The fact that our apartment was near all these places was great. It meant that the drunken, hungry staggers home—that characterized most weekends—were short. It also slimmed the probability of spending the night sharing cigarettes with a dirty bum (which you felt compelled to do because you were, after all, taking up space on a bench that was clearly his home).

Sometimes, we thought back to freshman year and laughed a lot. We laughed at how we never drank, we laughed at how we whispered scandal when Ziggy smoked up or offered us brownies. Once, he'd even offered me ten dollars if I ate just one piece from his pot-infused pan of dark, moist brownies. I'd been tempted because it looked so tasty, but had declined because it was laced with a drug and drugs were a gateway into an inescapable life of addiction-addled failure and misery.

When the munchies arrived, we headed to one of those roads that is a Springfield, a fixture throughout America. It's lined with gas stations and drive-thru windows—golden arches and neon Stetsons, a grinning hedgehog and Colonel Sanders. Broken Waffle House signs set the skyline and we spoke to metallic voices that sent our confused highs reeling into different worlds.

Hot paper bags of food in hand, we began the drive back home. We took a shortcut through the moneyed prettiness of Upper Arlington. The houses were big and brick and there were lush green breaks of colour—festive firs and hedge maple and hornbeams. It started to snow. We passed a church, more brick and stone houses, and I saw wreaths on doors. It looked like Christmas; it felt like childhood and home. I had lived this place before I ever lived here, and I felt warm, cocooned, connected.

That night, I am the kind of happy that is happiness just because it is; not excited about anything, not triumphant or relieved or grateful. Just happy, just plain happy. It is a very filling feeling. I feel full, like I am settled into leather, like my feet are dangling on cool marble and there are oozing eclairs and tandoori fries in the offing.

———

Eventually, we even tried to grow our own marijuana in Thomas's closet, with a heat lamp and frequent visits from smoking buddies who would take ponderous looks at the dying plant and prescribe a sure-shot remedy for curing it. In our desperation to save our plant-baby, whom we had christened Peggy Sue, we employed these remedies, every one of them.

We changed the soil, turned down the heat and turned up the heat, sprinkled it with bong water and crushed multivitamins over it. Peggy Sue finally withered to a brown crisp, and we extricated what little we could from her and sadly smoked that while ruining Elton John classics.

Goodbye, Peggy Sue
Though we barely got to smoke you at all
You were our child but we failed to raise you
Into a leafy green adult.

And it seems to us, you lived your life
Like a stoner without weed
Never growing into a full plant
Even when it rained multivitamins
And your twigs and remains will always stay
In the back of Tommy's closet
Your weedy-ness burned out long before
This damn heat lamp ever will.

# Bent

Campus had emptied out for winter break. I took the weekend
to sober up. Polo was coming to visit me for the holidays, and
I needed to protect my little brother from myself.

**Tara:** Distraction.

**Jay:** Hey, love. What's going on?

**Tara:** Trying to sober up before my brother gets
into town.

**Jay:** Haha, oh dear. And how is that going?

**Tara:** Not too terribly. I'm just drowning my sorrows
in Chipotle instead.

**Jay:** Tsk, tsk. What sorrows?

**Tara:** Blah, a boy.

**Jay:** :D

**Tara:** Stop laughing at me!

**Jay:** I'm not laughing at you. Well, I am, a little.

But only very fondly and not a little bit in exasperation.

**Tara:** I know, I know.

**Jay:** Sigh. Me too.

**Tara:** What're you up to?

**Jay:** Packing.
Panicking.

**Tara:** NYC?
April?

**Jay:** I know, I know.

**Tara:** Sigh. Jay.

**Jay:** It's the last attempt, dear girl.

**Tara:** And what if it doesn't work?

**Jay:** Then it doesn't work?

**Tara:** Really? Just like that?

**Jay:** Not at all. But the consequences are rather too awful for me to think about right now, if you don't mind.

**Tara:** Oh, I'm sorry!

**Jay:** Nothing to be sorry about ☺

**Tara:** ☹
Okay, I'll let you get back to packing. Thanks for the quick talk—it always brightens up my day ☺

Jay: Haha. Mm. You remind me of a song.

Tara: A song?

Jay: A good song.

Tara: Which one?

Jay: I try so hard to be good, to be good
I wish, I wish, if only I could

Tara: Mm. What song is that? I'm googling it to no avail.

Jay: Haha, you won't find it on Google. They only play it at this one shady little bar in London.

Tara: Who's they?

Jay: A ragged bunch of guys. Bad doctors, good ones, plumbers, painters, bankers, priests.

Tara: I'm going to go looking for it, someday.

Jay: You should ☺

———

Polo and I are both fond of being plonked into the centres of great, dirty, busy cities, so we went to Chicago. It was nearby, and it wasn't New York.

He is five years younger than me. He had always been a nice kid, and I think he might grow up to be a great man. I spent our childhood bullying him mercilessly, believing it an elder sister's birthright. Ever since I left home, though, some sort of distance-activated change had manifested itself, growing over time. Now, my insides twisted with affection when I watched his little head bobbing about in the pool and felt a fierce maternal instinct rise to panic when he came home nursing tennis injuries.

We stayed at the Ritz, an unremarkable building, smack in the midst of city bustle, looking out over The Magnificent Mile. You have to take an elevator up twelve floors to the lobby, which opens up to a vast expanse of tasteful gilt and creamy marble. One side is entirely lined with a huge bank of windows that soar to the ceiling and looks out over an endless sea of glass patched with sky.

On our first night there, Polo went to bed as soon as we returned to the hotel, tired from a day of cheering himself hoarse at Wrigley Field and exploring all the food in the city— deep-dish off the streets, unholy steak at the Ralph Lauren restaurant and cheesecake slices the size of small kittens. Sleep well, little brother, sleep calm, sleep deep and let all the restlessness straining inside my DNA never rear its ugly head in yours.

A storm broke, bending the building. A butler had come in to warn us about that right after we checked in. The taller buildings in the Windy City were engineered to move with the elements instead of against them, escaping the erosion of opposition.

They bent easily, but that's what kept them from breaking. I have held on to that fact. I try not to forget it, to keep it in mind, while counting steps and making Japanese flags.

I took an elevator down to the lobby to watch the storm thrash against the wall of windows. It brought to mind the note I'd written—to Jay, to me, to the universe—all those months ago (oh, but it had already been three years), after dancing to the music only we could hear.

Last night, you happened. Everything changed. I don't know how or why, but time will probably figure that stuff out.

For now, all I know, with a clarity surprising in its absoluteness, is I will grow to find you in all the places that call for me to feel deeply, to plumb my own depths.

I know I will think of you at every triumph, fleetingly but surely, and use you as a salve whenever I fail or am felled.

I know I'll feel you tingle in my fingers at the dignified howl of a piano playing Rachmaninoff and in the soaring plummet of my insides as planes take leave of the ground.

I know that, one day, I will stand warm-toed in the sand, on a shore, as a storm rages around me: as it lights up the sea and rings out the skies, validates and questions God. I know that I will miss you then, intensely, sharply, with a piercing feeling that is part need, part hurt, part love, part loss.

I know that there are years of this to pass. Years and years, wherein I will not be able to extricate you from the experiences that will shape me, make me. I will grow up with your unknowing spectre by my side, and I know someday our paths will—well, I'll hold on to a hope that they meet, not cross.

And I thought back to the dinner table at home a few days before I'd returned from summer break.

My mother had passed my dad the salad and said, 'The Sood cocktail is tomorrow.'

'I have to be in Delhi for a meeting. The Ghaziabad hotel hasn't been signed.'

'Can't you push it back for a day?'

He poured himself another measure of clear gold liquid, and I thought, just for an instant, that I saw a shadow flicker past my mother's face and settle in her eyes.

'No, dear, I can't. Aditya Dhillon doesn't hand out appointments at anyone else's convenience.'

A loud clatter told me I'd dropped my fork on the plate.

No one noticed. Or if they did, it wasn't important enough to comment upon.

Working hard to keep the frenetic contingency-building in my head off my face, I swallowed a sawdust bite of soft lamb and asked, 'Is he related to Vijay Dhillon?'

My dad turned to me, mildly surprised. 'Same family, different branch. This group owns the hotels and hospitals. The ones you're talking about are in shipping and real estate.'

'How do you know him, beta?'

I was prepared. I had spent enough time scouring for snippets about him online and in the papers to come up with a solid plausibility. 'Oh, he'd come to one of my SAT prep classes once, to tell us about college in America. He went to Yale or something. Some Ivy League place.'

My dad nodded and dressed his lamb clean off its bones. 'I've met him. He gave up his chair for me in the waiting room outside his uncle's office. Very polite boy.'

'Really? That's nice. I'm glad they had him come in and talk to you kids. You're all so competitive these days—

manners get left by the wayside, from everything I'm seeing.'

I excused myself from the table.

———

The thing was, I could have ceased aching for his perishable mind and the spread of his smile. But not his empathy, not his honour. I knew that—sitting at a table where everyone loved each other but no one knew how to talk to each other. I knew I could never shake him off.

And all the while, I was also trying to shake off the sudden, inexplicable face of a little girl—a little girl who had Jay's mouth and big, brown eyes—willing herself not to cry as shadows flickered and faded and settled on a cold mother's face around her.

# *Senior*

By the time junior year pulled to a close, we had stopped moving around in packs. We stopped pretending to be sad when returning home for the short winter breaks, and went to dinner without finding out whether every extended friend wanted to come along.

The summer before my last year of college commenced, I made the English major's requisite collegiate haj. A group of fellow students and I arrived at Heathrow for a summer study-abroad programme and piled into a bus bound for Stratford-upon-Avon.

Let me be clear. I like Shakespeare. I like his characters. I like the weight in some of his words and the cleverness in all of them. I enjoy being a groundling amidst the buzzing tourists inside The Globe, a fruity Pimm's in hand and *As You Like It* playing out on stage.

But do I like him or his work enough to sit through a week-long retrospective of various interpretations of *The Winter's Tale* by the (admittedly very talented) crew of the Royal Shakespeare Company? No. I don't. And apparently, neither did David or Ark. As I was sliding into sleep in the darkened theatre, an androgynous voice whispered in my ear, 'Hey, do you want to sneak out and drink at the pub down the road?'

God, yes.

I beamed a hell yeah at David. I'd vaguely recognized his face on the first day, when we'd all landed and met at Heathrow. In a minute, it clicked: he was the crazy guy everyone had seen taking a naked victory lap around campus the night that Obama won the 2008 elections. He completed the dash by jumping into Glass Lake in the throes of a Midwestern November. It said something about the magnitude of that moment in our time, I think, that he became a sort of mini-hero around campus for a while thereafter. If there was ever a day for our generation to streak into an icy lake in beholden thanks, that was it.

The three of us left the theatre in identical second-short slivers of light through an exit in the back. Outside, I learned that Ark, who bore a comical resemblance to Bill Cosby, was just taking the trip to fulfil a Humanities requirement for his physics major and couldn't take another minute of Shakespeare without a fortifying haze.

We went to The Dirty Duck, which, as David had whispered, was just down the road. British pubs have such fantastic names—The Dirty Duck, The Soiled Pig, Wolf & Marrow, and, here and there, The Slug and Lettuce. This one had a dirt floor, furniture that looked like it had been hewed by hand before the Norman Conquest and an overgrown outdoor patio that the word 'picturesque' was coined after in 1592. The three of us settled into the patio and went through two bottles of their house wine. They brought the bottles out in a rusty steel pail, which put us all in a very good mood.

By the time the rest of our group finished their session for the day and came looking for us, we were rolling around in the grass, clanking empty bulbs and singing Auld Lang Sine.

Cliques are to large groups of people what awkward moments are to attempted ménage à trois—they're going to happen, no two ways about it.

David, Ark and I formed a cosy band. We kept it easy. Drank a lot, ate a bunch of animal innards, smoked some British pot, drank some more. The three of us were also, to the undisguised (and understandable) displeasure of some of the others, at the top of the class. As part of our study-abroad experience, we had to pursue a month of academia in an English college. This required a substantial deal more learning by rote and technical research (as opposed to being resourceful and venturing opinions) than your standard American liberal-arts classes call for. Close on fifteen years of a formidable Indian education had taught me how to circumvent putting my nose anywhere near a grindstone even when those behemoths of academic pressure— the ICSE and ISC—loomed large (the answers are always in the question paper, in case you were wondering). David had grown up in embassies around the world, studying under the regimented umbrella of the International Baccalaureate, and Ark was just some gorgeous freak of nature. So while the pure-bred Americans worked on their British homework, we went to Paris and stayed in Montmartre, at a hotel with an old-fashioned manual elevator and an angry transgender French maid who grumbled displeasure every time one of us said something in our pronounced American accents, 'comme des imbeciles'.

Over Strongbow one night, I felt brave enough to tell David and Ark about Jay. They were sympathetic. And no, no I couldn't say anything while he had a girlfriend.

'Guys. I need to go look for something.'

Ark took a swig while nodding. 'Sure. We'll all go. What do you need to find?'

'A song?'

David looked delighted. 'Explain!'

'So, a long time ago, well, two months or more, anyway, Jay told me about this song that you can only find here. He quoted some lyrics, said I made him think of them, and when I tried to look up the song, he said they only play it in some bar here. I want to, well, I suppose I want to find the song.'

We walked through London, entering bars at random and asking after the lyrics. It was an aimless quest, of course, indubitably ill-fated when it came to fulfilment, and after a couple of hours, I said, 'It's okay. We're done. I just needed to look for it.'

David looked me straight in the eye and told me he thought I was the freest person he had ever met, an absolute hedon, and that he wanted to embrace life like I did. I looked at his half-head of pink hair and sad, sad eyes and wished it were true, then hoped that maybe it was.

Outside, the sky was dusty with light. Leicester Square was sending a thousand twinkles up into the air and we walked under the diffused glow of them all, tracing our steps on to the streets of London. I idly wondered, perhaps out loud, whether the ground was an alive thing, whether every foot that fell upon it was an invisible line left like so many words and kisses and bruises on our bodies. Whether it needed our tread upon it, the way we needed to be touched. Without us walking it, would the ground fall away? Would it cease to live?

David held my hand.

Near Piccadilly, three storeys of a building reverberated with an inviting bass, and we held our breath.

I turned to David. 'Are we drunk enough?'

'I am. Are you?'

'Yeah, I think so. Ark?'

'Let's do this.'

There are always an initial few moments of jolted apprehension when you step into a club. It's dark and loud and filled with people, all of whom look beautiful until you look at them in the light. But we adapt quickly. We drink more drinks and get closer to the music and turn into one of the beautiful people ourselves.

*Well I just dance the way I feel*

We had segued into our environs and lost each other. I was standing with a nameless boy, and I kind of wanted to push his hand off my hip but I didn't. He said something. I got distracted watching his blonde hair skim the rims of his eyes, getting irritated by the fact that he wasn't brushing the offending locks away, then remembered to smile a vague assent. Thank God for the rules. Thank God for this game.

He smiled too, and shook his head, pointing up at the ceiling in the somehow-universal gesture referring to the music being played, and said in a louder voice, 'Good song, yeah?'

I nodded and leaned my lips into his ear. 'Ou Est le Swimming Pool.'

He continued the exchange of leanings-in. 'You French, yeah? Dishy.'

I started to laugh—and then changed my mind.

'Oui.'

I didn't lean all the way out. We kissed. And it was something, so when I felt teeth on my lips and tongue in my mouth, I went along with it. Why not, yeah?

*Stop*

We broke for a breath after a few minutes and, as I pushed away the hair that had fallen all around my face, I said, 'That was all very sudden.'

*Well I just dance the way I feel*

What little I could see of his face looked confused. 'All right? You want to do this or not?'

All I could see were the watery blue of his vacant eyes and I tried to not, tried to form a picture of an undashed possibility—dark eyes and tousled hair, words and words and words—but it eluded me and, somehow, I was looking at a hesitant smile in a pink lehenga.

No.

'I need another drink.'

*Stop breathing*

'Course.'

'I should probably find my friends first, though—'

He gestured to one of the black couches lining the dark walls, where Ark was obscured by expanses of white leg and red hair.

I sent David a text asking him where he was, and nodded at the guy. For the first time, I noticed he was wearing a blue jumper and made a mental note to keep at least that in mind.

He guided me through the tightly packed bodies, all of them dancing or drinking or kissing or crying, to the slammed bar on the ground floor. There was his hand on the small of my back and sometimes, the brush of his mouth along my neck, and I tried to feel all the things I wanted to feel, I really did.

I drank something disgusting. A cocktail of different liquors, intended only for the purpose of quick obliteration.

Quickly, the boy became a beat between my legs and a whisper in my ear—'Shall we?'

No.

'Yup. Your place.'

*Imagine none of this is real*

His apartment was in one of those buildings where you have to walk past judgmental eyes that track you down the lobby to the elevators at the end. It was the only point during the evening where I felt I would unravel, where I felt like walking up to the person attached to the eyes and ask them if they could help me, could they help me please, because I didn't know what I was doing and all I was trying to do was forget, and I judge me too, sir, I do. But I just need to forget, just for a while.

Inside his moderately neat bedroom, I worked hard. I concentrated on not thinking. It took a lot of effort to stay there, in that moment, in that apartment, with that boy. I was lightly exhausted even before there was any reason to be.

Is this the best kind of sex? The kind that's all about you, only about you. He doesn't matter. He isn't even really there.

It's all in the mind, isn't it?

Appearances.

It's in the perfectly timed arch of a back and nails that hurt just enough to feel good, to feel like she's lost control. It's a cry brushed up against an ear so the sound is tactile, soft lips grazing a soft lobe. It's holding a gaze right before she slow-shuts her eyes and bows her head back, showing you the hollow at the bottom of her neck where the beats of her heart are recorded. She's lost control, you think—God yes, come for me, damn that feels good.

And you feel your power surge through you and out of you and you put it in me, desperately, and can't you see that it's my hands and my eyes and my tongue on your skin that's doing this?

Not you. Never you. You're nothing. It's always him, and I should apologize to you, but you wouldn't want me to.

All I have to do is pretend to lose control and, because you are a man, you believe it your due, you accept that you can do this to me. But the reins will always be in my hands and your fucking world will be in my mouth. This is a flawlessly executed play, and you lie back and your chest is level with the surface of the nightstand and then it's rising to the top of the alarm clock. Nightstand-alarm clock-nightstand-alarm clock-nightstand-alarm clock.

'Fuck.' His voice is just threads. 'Fuuuuuuuuck.'

Please don't touch me. Please don't touch me.

But, of course, you're going to sit up and shake your head and hold me and say something nice and I'm going to want to throw up but settle for shrugging out of your hard, sick embrace.

'Do you have a cigarette?'

'I don't smoke, love.'

I blanched. 'Okay, well, I need to go out and get some. It was nice meeting you.'

'I'll walk you out, yeah?'

'No, you won't.'

He looked confused, again. This is all I would remember

of him, this confused expression and the blue jumper that was now lying on the floor.

'You could sleep here tonight, if you wanted to.'

'Jesus, man. Get a hold of yourself. Bye.'

Later that night, I watched morning break to Ou Est le Swimming Pool's only album on repeat, while smoking half a pack up and down the Thames Path. For a while, I felt the water whisper to me, saying it wouldn't be that bad, that it takes lungs only a moment to fill up. And then, then it's just a soft, sweet embrace.

————

Back at school in America, David, Ark and I continued to hang out on a basis frequent, enough to make us good friends without throwing us into the intensity and inevitable drama of being close friends.

The two of them were calm guys. Stark individuals, which made them, in my eyes, hella cool. David was obsessed with learning to cook Ethiopian food and Ark was studying Holography; he told us how every point on a hologram contains the entire image, and it's one of those random facts that I'll never quite stop thinking about because of the hidden profundity there that's lying just out of reach.

They were interesting people, and also an interested audience. Interested in a way that telling them about my day or life felt like writing in a journal—the information would be absorbed, I would feel better. No attempts to help me or fix my life would be made because they weren't trying to impress me, had no reason to truss me with a greater purpose in mind. They would simply not judge me. They would listen to what I had to say, and silently care about it, because they were my friends. David and Ark were the only truly non-sexual straight male friends my own age I have ever had, the only two completely platonic relationships with people who fit the bill for 'non-platonicity'.

Well, that's not entirely true.

———

It seemed that even our fifty-thousand-student-strong campus could, much like the shrunken millions of my home city, seem like a very small place. As it were, it turned out that David and Jane were fast friends, smoking buddies. We only discovered this as Jane and I were having breakfast on campus one day, and David chanced upon us in the course of his morning coffee run.

It was a genuinely pleasant surprise for people who genuinely all liked each other. By then, we were all established potheads, and our gatherings led to a variety of small ventures that felt like big adventures because we were blazed throughout them.

Often, we sat around at Jack's and often, David said, 'Let's go to Narnia.'

Narnia is a secret garden, hollowed out in the main quad of our campus. A right at the outdoor amphitheatre, a duck into a shrubbered path behind Glass Lake, and you're in a secluded little vale, a leafy green grotto filled with the sweet smell of foliage just taking to rot.

That night, it's Jane, David, Ark, Thomas (who'd come

along because he had what I'd assured him was a pointless crush on the heterosexual David) and me in Narnia.

We sat on the melting grass, we got wet olive stains on our jeans and our Chucks (Jane wore purple, David wore teal, I wore sequined black). We packed and smoked my handblown pink-and-yellow pipe. I had found the piece a few months ago in the expected run-down thrift shop run by an unexpected man in a suit and tie and frown. We spent a lot of time looking at it, passing it around, taking turns to smoke it and look at it and comment on it. Whoever made it did beautiful work. The lines bloomed in clean curves. Fluid, restrained lines. And, inside those simple lines, the glass turned into pink and yellow swirls. There were places where the yellow deepened into turning beads of gold, curling indentations, the night settling pale gold on our fingers.

Ark looked at me and asked, 'So hey, Tara, how long have you been smoking? Because I remember, when I first saw you, it was like, what, two years ago? When you were Jane's roommate in Honour Hall? And I remember, you didn't smoke at all back then, did you?'

'Wait, what? You were in our room?'

'Yeah, lots of times! I was in there so often!'

'How do I not remember this?'

He laughed. 'You were hardly ever there, maybe that's why.'

David giggled, 'Big man, Tars, important girl.'

'This is crazy. I can't believe I don't remember you from our room.'

'Yeah you were, you were usually gone.'

'Yeah, I was out breaking shit. It wasn't such a good year for me.'

Jane hmm'd in agreement. 'Yeah ... You were crying all the time. And fuck, you and Asher, like seriously, you guys were drinking all the time. Like, all. The. Time. I'd wake up and you guys would be spiking your Starbucks'.

'You'd join us every time!'

'Of course I did, girl! Morning beverages are the best.'

Ark persevered, 'So when did you start smoking?'

'Earlier this year, I think. Yeah. Well it's been, what, like ten months now, I'd say.'

'Really? You already smoke like a pro, girl.'

'Hey, what I lack in experience I make up in regularity, homie.'

It was only funny because we were high, but man, did we find that funny. Hysterical laughter, re-voicing the exchange, and then, when we were laughing too hard to speak, miming it with slow hands and scrunched faces.

We didn't stop until Jane shushed us because a squirrel had scuttled up behind David and she didn't want to scare it away. Jane loves squirrels. And all other animals of furry persuasions.

It looked up in the sudden hush. Paused for a second, let out a squeak, dropped the nut in its hand, and ran away. It occurred to me with what felt like life-changing clarity that the squirrel's demeanour was a lot like Thomas's.

'Geez, I kind of feel like we have to take that personally, Jane.'

'Shut up, Tars, we scared the poor little guy.'

Ark said, 'I'm okay with scaring a squirrel, man. Did I ever tell you about the squirrel situation the year I lived with Steve up on Neil? I told you right, David?'

'Yeah, you told me.'

'I didn't tell you guys though, did I? Okay, so listen. I guess there was this squirrel living in Steve's room and it died? And it decayed and it smelled so, so bad in there. Like, we could smell it all the way downstairs in the kitchen when we were cooking and shit. And we went on searching for this horrible smell all the time and we finally found it right at the end of the year. That fucking squirrel, it had probably been dead for so long, man. We had to cut a hole in his closet, because it was inside his closet and we couldn't find the smell so we had to cut a hole, like right into his drywall, to find it. It was disgusting . . .' He trailed off and started digging the ends of his undone shoelace into the grass.

David laughed and said, 'This is coming from the same kid who used to catch spiders and eat them.'

Jane made a puking sound. 'That's really gross.'

'No man, I used to work at this restaurant back in high school and the umbrellas and tables and stuff outside were, like, fine during the day, but I don't know what it was, at night the spiders would come out like crazy. Like, everything would just be full of spiders. Tables, chairs, umbrellas, everything—just crawling with them. And they were some of the juiciest spiders I've ever seen, man. Like their juicy part was an inch thick, no joke. So that's all I ate, just the juicy part, man.'

I heard someone mumble, 'That's messed up, that's real messed up.'

'No dude, those spiders had meat on their bones. I'm telling you. And they were everywhere. Like sometimes they'd fall in the water and you'd just watch them die.'

No one said anything for a while. I think we were all thinking about what a drowning spider would look like. I know I was.

Ark, who had seen it and didn't have to build the scene piecemeal in his imagination, spoke again. 'Like, spiders are, I don't know, man, just, like, so terrifying, to such an enormous population. Like, socially and mentally. I guess a lot of people hate spiders. I mean, I ate them but I still hate them, man. I've hated spiders since I was a child. Just, you know, how they are. I dislike them as members of life on earth. Spiders and bees. But with bees I have my personal reasons, like being stung and stuff. Spiders, I just dislike because they're spiders.'

My voice said, 'Well, that makes sense though. Just think about a spider's basic mode of survival, you know. Like, it perfectly fits our social narrative of creepy-stalker-killer man.'

Other voices agreed with that for a while and then mine came out again. 'I want to know where David and Thomas went, that's what I want to know. Where did they go?'

'Oh yeah, hey, when did they leave?'

'I don't know, let's go look for them.'

Legs asleep, we groaned to our feet and brushed broken blades of grass off our jeans. There was nothing to be done about the olive stains and we just had to feel their clinging wetness.

Outside Narnia, the quad stretched in a giant circle around us. We started walking around slowly.

'Oh shit—look!'

Following the motion of Ark's head, we saw David pushed up against a tree, face thrown back into relief and eyes closed as Thomas, on his knees, pressed his face into his crotch and turned his blonde head this way and that.

I laughed, understanding.

We watched them for a minute or two and then, hungry,

went to find food. McDonalds was the only place open that late, so we got greasy burgers, greasy fries and sugary strawberry milkshakes.

———

They lie, you know. They try to scare us. It's not the leaves and the powders and the pills that are addictive. Our bodies talk, they tell us what's up. They shake a hand and swim a head when we've had enough. They squirt fear and project mothers' faces into brains when voluntary play begins to slip away. We get the hints, we are forewarned. After that, it's a choice. And like at any overstocked American supermarket, we are absolutely spoilt for choice.

If you want the powder too much, smoke the leaves. If the leaves are getting the better of you (though marijuana is not a physically addictive substance, so it really can't do that) then crush a pill. As a general rule of thumb, anything that comes in a needle is best left alone. We don't go down that road.

There is not one among all of us who spent junior and senior year smokingsnortingdrinkingfuckingup who did not go on to clean up, to professional success and mortgages and sensible shoes and tattoos only high up arms and legs, where employers can't see them. We did all that, and now we do all this. And God knows if the others want to go back to Narnia the way I do, sometimes. Only sometimes. But we have mortgages and bosses, and salad for dinner, and it's okay. It's all okay.

Addiction is a choice. It is in the mind, a state of mind. We need something to do, and we can do anything.

*Together togethertogethertogether*

## May

It had just started raining outside, and I had worked up the nerve to talk to Jay.

It had been six months and seventeen days since we last spoke.

Six plus one plus seven is fourteen, one plus four is five, and five is a good number.

I have to talk to him. I have to remind him I exist.

I logged in to various social media services every day, to check if he was around. I worried if he wasn't.

But you were there today, a little green dot, and I worked up the nerve to talk to you because it had been too long, it had been half a year, and I missed you so terribly.

**Tara:** Hello, how goes all?

**Jay:** Tired, most of the time.
How are you doing?

**Tara:** Same. I love it. ☺

**Jay:** Haha, and where are you?

**Tara:** Junior year at school
Where are you?

**Jay:** Delhi, India

**Tara:** Ahh my favourite city!
Aight, I'll let you go. Just wanted to check in
and see if the Mr Dhillon lives on ☺

**Jay:** Haha, he lives on and is happy.
Stay with me, just a little, just for a while,
before our cursory conversation is over and I have
to wait another year to make contact.

**Tara:** I thought of you recently when I was editing
college application essays for my brother and
23649298 of his friends

**Jay:** Hahahaha, welcome to my world!

**Tara:** I liked it! Now I know all the deep, dark
secrets and desires of so many people! Good times.

**Jay:** Mm.You know the fake deep dark secrets they
choose to reveal to make themselves look more
appealing. The real stuff as we all know is well
suppressed or well hidden. Usually under mounds
of shame, guilt and insecurity.

**Tara:** Oh stop besting me and go away.

**Jay:** I do have the advantage in experience and
age . . . God I feel old!

**Tara:** Haha, you should! I just turned 21 and I feel ancient!

**Jay:** Sigh . . . I'm over the hill.

**Tara:** Shaadi kab hai, Uncleji?☺

**Jay:** Oh God, don't even mention that! I'm going down the arranged-marriage route—not a pretty process.

**Tara:** Oh dear. And how's that going?

**Jay:** Terrible! More and more, the universe is telling me that I may have to settle.
I really, truly want to feel that the person whom I marry is too good for me. I suspect, when everything fails, despite appearances, the opposite may happen.

**Tara:** Haha, you must give me an anecdote.

**Jay:** Sigh. Let me think of a good one.
Oh yes! There was this one girl, great family, great background. Greatest achievement is driving the family Rolls, social life relegated to her cousins and nephews, claims to love art but doesn't know her Caravaggio from her Dali, claims to love reading but couldn't name three authors she liked when I asked. Argh!

**Tara:** Can I ask you something in the most non-judgemental way possible?
Why're you doing this? I mean, you travel the world, you meet a million fascinating people. How can socialites from south Delhi entice you?

**Jay:** Sigh. When I tell that to people they call me an arrogant ass.
**Tara:** Please, keep your arrogance. It's hot. You, of all people, should have a good story.

———

I thought of this girl—of all the girls—being introduced to you. They'd known you as a name and a link on some chain of people their families knew. I thought of the you they'd see. The immaculate cut of suit, the permanent tousle of hair, the sudden downturn of nose. I wondered if they spent time thinking about the array of your smiles—the quick one that is mischief all over your face, the wide one that is a pose for the camera, the slow, spreading one that turns your eyes lazy. I wondered whether they could sense how singular you are, how you're a kid in a boardroom and a man in a hoodie, how the alleys of your mind are patrolled by a savant debauched in the dark. And I wondered, I wondered with true wonder, how they could wait to find out everything about you. How they could restrain themselves from asking you what you find beautiful, what moves you, hurts you, shakes you, breaks you.

I wanted to know. I'd always wanted to know. And you'd never told me. Because I never asked, it's true. But how could I?

What was it that Radiohead said?

I'm a creep, I'm a weirdo, I wish I was special.

I'm drunk and I'm pissed and *you're so fucking special*.

# *Florence's Graceless Heart*

Mark's frenzied thrusting was making my Mary Poppins headboard pound against the wall, and all I could think about was the marks it would leave on the paint. We had met while my ears were ringing at some loud club, but stripped of vodka and smoke and Guetta, heat and chemistry were replaced by a slobbering tongue two inches off target and excruciatingly unenticing animal jerks. I tried to concentrate on the fact that, from certain angles, he was a dead ringer for that hot-boss guy on *Ugly Betty*. But ecstasy had rendered his face ugly; scrunched up and gasping, he repulsed me.

'Okay, we're done. Get off me.'

He looked dazed. 'Huh, what?'

'This isn't working for me right now, sorry.'

Then, because he said nothing, 'Sorry.'

Shit, that didn't really sound genuine. Oh well.

'Tara, what's wrong?'

The hurt concern in his voice made me recoil even further. Recoil to the point, in fact, that I then sprung out, straight towards anger. At what exactly, I don't know. I mean, it was ostensibly because he had ruined what could have been a night of fun and then, instead of coming up with some redeeming, igniting rage of his own, squelched whatever chance there was of resurrecting lust with a cold dollop of greasy saccharine. But I couldn't be that, that, well, whatever—selfish, irreverent, base, insensate—could I? At least not demonstrably so, no.

I wimped out and bowed to humanity's goddamn code of conduct.

'It's just— I just have a lot on my mind, Mark.'

'Oh okay, I see. It's not really me, is it, babe?' His voice softened, tendered. 'You just don't want to get even more attached and then have to leave.'

Apparently overwhelmed by emotion, he honed in for a hug. Ducking, I stroked his chest and pretended to sniffle. At least he had perfect abs. I recalled him saying something about being a physical trainer; guess that explained it.

'Yeah, and you know, I only have a couple of months left here. So, yeah.'

'It's just two months now?'

About seven, actually, but he didn't need to know that. 'Mmhm. I'm graduating early.'

'Well, know that there is a heart here that already misses you very much.'

Miraculously, the welling urge to retch got expelled as a sob-like sound.

After he left, I sent Asher a text:

Who decided being kind to people was more important than being good in bed?

He replied with a laughing emoticon and an instruction to meet him at Jack's in fifteen.

We came out in our Halloween best. The Lady of Shallot, a sexy ringmaster, white Grace Jones and a horse.

Asher and Jane had found a deserted children's amusement park that was housing an all-night rave. The inappropriateness of it sat nicely with us, so Darya and I forked over a hundred dollars and stepped in.

I was nervous. Jane was on Asher's back.

A hard-bodied Atlas threw his beach-ball-world at me. 'Catch!'

I turned to the ringmaster. 'Darya, I need a drink. Or something.'

Asher said, 'We drink all the time. Let's look for Molly.'

Jane asked, 'How do we get it? We can't just go up to people and ask for drugs.'

'Why not?'

'Because if there's a cop around, we get arrested, Tara.'

'Oh.'

Darya knew. 'What you do is go up to people who look like they might have something and ask if they've seen your friend Molly.'

'Cool.'

I was glad I didn't also have to ask how to spot someone who might have something. That part was easy. That part was the too-happy eyes, and skin that looked cold. That part was the girl licking glitter off a centaur's body and the topless cowboy riding Shrek.

We separated. We went to look for Molly.

I walked past crumbling roller coasters draped with glowing ghouls, past empty ice-cream shops with grinning pumpkins in the windows. Past a funnel-cake stand that I wished was open for business.

There were groups of people, of Elvises and Gagas and slutty kitties and Harry Potters, who were going wild, who would definitely know where to find Molly. But I was afraid to go up to them, so I didn't.

I saw a very tall boy standing alone next to the water slides.

He's shaking, he's loaded. 'Nice costume.'

'It's not a costume.'

'Were you—'

'Yeah. For six months.'

'Where?'

'Stop it.'

'What?'

'Iraq.'

'Really?'

'What're you looking for?'

Right. 'Um, have you seen my friend Molly?'

'I don't have uncut. Just pills.'

'What's it cut with?'

'Just caffeine.'

'Okay, how much?'

'Eighty bucks.'

'For one?'

'For one.'

'That's too much.'

'Eighty bucks.'

'Dude, they're supposed to go for fifteen a pop, tops.' Darya would never have sent us off without a comprehensive relay of information.

'Look, I . . . I get it as part of a study, okay? Safety's guaranteed.'

'What do you mean? What kind of study?'

'I dunno. They're giving this stuff to some of us who came back different, as an experiment.'

I'd read about these experiments, I think. About the soldiers who came back and screamed their neighbours awake every night and needed to be medicated, sedated, put away, locked away. They were given little pills and pouches of powder to escape from the war that would not release them, little pills of Ex and pouches of pure-cut MDMA.

'I need four—no, five.'

'Four hundred.'

Four Benjamins. Five little white pills.

I called Asher. 'Got it.'

'Awesome. How—no, we're good. Jane, c'mon, let's go—how many?'

'One for each of us.'

'Great. Meet you at the haunted house in five.'

'Wait, where is that?'

'Where are you?'

'By the water slides.'

'Okay wait there. We're coming to get you.'

They came and got me. We went into a dark, cavernous space streaked with remains of melty-faced amputees and asylum escapees, where plastic pop-ups shaped like the rising undead used to give chase to screaming kids who made a run for it, only to be greeted by a pointy Nosferatu at the next turn.

I handed the pills to Jane and she said, 'We should snort these. It'll hit us faster.'

Asher pulled out his phone and I crushed the pill with the butt of mine and on to its smooth mirror back. It was easy, no different from crushing up the Adderall we snorted on nights before a big exam or a big party. We sat in the haunted house, and we had an iPhone covered in Halloween goodies.

Darya used her credit card to slice up the small mound of white powder into even lines. It took a lot more time than we expected. She wanted them to be perfect. Other people stumbled into the privacy of the hollowed-out haunted house, but they didn't care about us and we didn't care about them. They threw up and passed out and made out, and Darya cut the lines, evened out the lines.

'Who has a dollar?'

'Mm, I have a fifty.'

'Excellent, we do this in style.'

'Roll it tight, Tara.'

'This good?'

'Just tighten it up a bit more. Yeah, that's good.'

I held up the fifty-dollar tube. 'Who wants to go first?'

It might as well have been baby powder, those lines. So finely ground, so soft to the touch, acquiescing, melting, yours if only you'll have it. All the good it needed to promise was really just *anything* else, any escape, anything different from the banality, from the sheer nothingness of being given this life. This life with nothing but pre-ordered restraints and suffocating little cubes for us to live in. We are born into jails, jailed in by heavens and hells, by right and wrong, black and white, grey-isn't-really-a-colour, we have no control, no say, can't you see? And everything we do to get away from it, every visit to the bottom of every bottle, every joint and blunt and pipe eventually dulls away back into reality. Unacceptable, untenable, limited, hopeless reality.

'My neurons are so happy . . .'

And Asher said, 'I check the missed connections personals on Craigslist every day, but no one ever looks for me.'

So I'll breathe in this baby powder, and like a baby, have something to wonder at. A world shinier and happier and, most of all, at least a little new. I will speed up, my pulse will slow down, the music will sound better. I'll feel something. We'll go to a club, we'll go to a dozen clubs, and we'll drink and we'll dance and we won't even really get drunk because we're already so high, and it will be wonderful. It will be wonderful. It has to be wonderful. And there, underneath the Herculean beats and lying lights, underneath this desperate, fake intimacy, this will be my salvation.

———

I lay hung-over in bed as my phone buzzed. A text message from Mark.

I think I might be getting a cold.

Goddammit, he was going to whine again. Reluctantly, I texted him back.

Fluids! Sleep! Chicken soup! Pre-emptive meds!

Come and make me soup then. I already slept and took Dayquil.

Haha. I would if I could:)

You owe me a dinner for that time you didn't show up for the one at my place ☺

That dinner had been the cause of one of our big fights, the one that had ended things the last time in a long list of recurring times. Classes, exams and research papers are enough to keep anyone busy, but I had extensive rounds of the bars to do every night as well. I had cancelled on Mark several times over the course of our two-month relationship, and he finally got pissed when I didn't show up for a special dinner he had pencilled me in for weeks in advance. I used that opportunity to pick a big fight and call off the relationship. Then I boarded the plane to India boyfriend-free and only slightly guilty, the diamond necklace he had given me as an early Christmas present sitting heavy in my bag. The necklace was beautiful, a dainty little heart encrusted with diamonds dangling from a gossamer-like silver chain. It was also something I would never wear—the diametric opposite of the oversized glass cocktail rings and feathers on thread I always wore.

And you want to waste that on chicken soup?

Absolutely. You taking care of me when I'm sick and making me chicken soup? So worth it. Bonus points if you can make me a grilled cheese sammich too ☺

I knew what I wanted to say. For one, stop talking to me like I'm your girlfriend. And stick your grilled cheese sammich where the sun doesn't shine, please.

I hated what he was doing. Trying to be cute, employing sass and coquettishness to impress the object of his affections. It revolted me.

Yeah, well. I have to go get this paper done.

You always have to get something done. And on the blue moon that I do get to see you, there are all

these crazy rules I'm supposed to be following like
taking you home at five in the morning because you
apparently can't sleep in the same bed as someone
else. You can't treat me like this just because
I'm in love with you, Tara.

Ugh.

Ugh.

Drunk and bored later that night, I lay in bed mindlessly
scrolling through Facebook. It's fucking Disneyland in there.
The happiest fucking place on earth. It's like a race to see who
can make their lives appear the most fun. A contest where
the person posting about absolute banalities with the highest
number of exclamation points wins. I'm sure it was great getting
off work twenty minutes early, but what sort of uninformed
narcissism makes you think all seven hundred and twenty-two
of your friends need to know exactly how pumped you were
when that happened?

I stalked Jay's profile, like I always did when I was lonely.
Nothing new, as usual. I spent an hour looking through his
old photos. The pictures of him sailing the Riviera with some
stunning companions finally drove me away.

Fuck you.

I went and got another drink. Clear Belvedere in a water-
spotted wine bulb.

Thomas had been yelling at me to do the dishes, but I knew
that if I waited long enough, he would just do them himself.

Morose, I looked for the small, selfish comfort of being
wanted.

Actual conversation would have been too much at that

point, so I went to Mark's profile page, to look at pictures of and posts from someone who loved me. I did sort of want to call him, but he would've been asleep by then. That's what normal people do at three in the morning.

I stared blankly at his profile picture for a while, trying not to see a dark hand around a fair waist by the saturated blue of expensive waters.

Five hours ago, he had changed his Facebook status:

You should learn how to show your feelings so I know what to do with mine.

―――――

For a few minutes every day, I put on a ramrod pretence—I-am-not-drunk, I-am-not-high, I-am-not-fucked-up—and I talked to my mother—is-everything-okay and yes-yes-not-to worry all around.

'Okay, great. Talk to you later, then, Mom. Need to get to class.'

'Hold on, I need to talk to you about something. Nitwit is engaged.'

'Good for her.'

'You don't need to use that tone.'

'What? It *is* good for her. It's what she's been angling for since she hit puberty.'

'Well, anyway, you're going to have to come with me to Delhi for her *roka*.'

'What's a roka?'

'It's like an engagement ceremony. Makes things official.'

'So the groom can't escape?'

'Tara, stop it.'

'Ugh, Mom. Do I have to?'

'Yes, beta. She specifically called and asked when you'd be in India and organized her dates accordingly.'

'Fine, fine.'

———

It had been seventeen months since the brownies. I didn't remember most of it.

That moment of falling prey to addiction is a funny one. It sneaks up on you in the middle of a coffee run, and splashes burns on to your fingers because you can't hold them steady. It hurts. It hurts like crazy, and you hope no one saw it happen.

Hell, I didn't see it happen.

You realize that when you stood drunk outside a party and, hopped up on American acceptance and full of self-imposed existential angst, declared between drags of a cigarette that 'I could really use a line right now', you were full of all kinds of shit.

But I could really use a line right now.

———

Everything I've ever loved is battered, cracked, used up. *A Little Princess* is splintered at the spine, the margins are bleeding conversations with Burnett, and almost every page has a dog-eared indentation. The Row's black leather leggings are worn to their thready bones. My knee is shredded from too much Lock & Key, and bruises bite the terrain along my neck and breasts and stomach. My body has been touched, hurt, burnt, stretched, shunned, loved. I inhabit this decaying shell, and because I cannot save it, I use it.

As if on cue, David texted me:

```
I keep taking bong rips so big that I stop
breathing and my body freaks out coz it thinks
it's dying. How fucked up is that?
```

I replied:

```
It's beautiful. Use your body; there's no sense
in preserving something that's already dying. ☺
```

# Glitter in the Blow

I was writing in my room, waiting for Button and Cookie to make requisite token appearances at their respective homes before heading back over. I was in India only for two weeks and in Calcutta for a mere fraction of that, so we had to make the days count. The rest of my last winter vacation at home was to be spent in Delhi, attending Nitwit's roka and spending time with the relatives I'd happily ignored for the better part of three and a half years.

Polo walked in, his dog, Roger Fedora, wagging beside him. 'I want food.'

'Me too. Button and Cookie should be coming over any time now. Let's go to Blue China?'

'Yeah, Bozey should be here in a few minutes too.'

'Why didn't he just come straight home with you after school?'

'He's at some coding competition.'

'What's coding?'

'How are you so dumb?'

'Please. You're illiterate.'

'Balls.'

'Name four books you've read.'

There was a hammer-heavy knock on the door and Bozey appeared. Next to Roger Fedora, he was my brother's best friend. A large, hulking drummer, who I heard had girls screaming for him at school fests. This generation's Kage, I thought, smiling sagely at the wry wisdom of my advanced years. 'She's got you there, bro.'

Polo grinned at him. 'How did it go?'

'Not too bad. We came second.'

'Don't tell me those shitheads at St Jude's won again?'

'Yeah.'

'Shitheads.'

Still curious about this coding business, I redirected my query at Bozey, barely grasping anything he said.

'It sounds like sci-fi! So, what, you guys just sit there typing up a storm for hours and then stuff happens?'

'No, no, we just coded for, like, half an hour. Basic shit. We had to sit through a long-ass speech by some Vijay Dhillon guy first. He's supposed to be a genius coder or something.'

I tempered back my squeal to a coughing fit. Focus, focus. Scavenge now, savour later.

Bozey seemed sceptical about the veracity of the Princeton degree Jay 'claimed to have' and quirked a sarcastic laugh at the American accent he presumed he was faking. I forgave him that because he was seventeen. Seventeen, and smart. Secure in the knowledge that his is a complete, comprehensive view of the world and everything in it. Besides, there was no time to be mad. I had to play it cool and get more details out of him.

Fortunately, an unwitting Polo came to my aid. 'So basically, it all sucked. Can we go eat now?'

'Actually, no, this dude turned out to be cool as hell, man. You know how lame these fucking speeches always are. Like, just let us get to the fucking code-off, fuckers.'

I threw a cushion at his head. 'Watch your language, Bozey.'

Surprisingly, he looked chastened. 'Sorry, Tars.'

He went all quiet after apologizing and, cursing myself for interrupting whatever he had been saying about Jay, I scrambled to bring him back to it. Said, in as casual a voice as I could, 'Anyway, what were you saying about the dude and the speech thing?'

'Oh yeah, that. Nothing really. Just that it turned out to be the best chief-guest speech I've ever heard.' He sat up, betraying excitement. 'Yeah, so this dude, like, official-looking dude, right? He talked about 4chan and asked us all these questions about cloud computing and *Pirates of the Silicon Valley*. It was great! I stayed awake through the whole thing!'

Only you.

I felt a burst of the best kind of pride. The kind that cracks open your whole face into a giant smile so big that you feel it in the tips of your fingers and toes, every muscle in your body coming to the party. Little things like this verified everything I had suspected about him from the beginning. And that verification felt great. It reaffirmed my faith in myself, because I saw this, I sensed this, I picked this. I picked him and he was incredible.

I paused for a moment to hope that there was someone in his life—a friend, a brother, a girlfriend—to give him a high five or a long, fierce kiss in acknowledgement of his achievements. I was too happy and thrilled for him to even care that I was not the one allowed to tell him—congratulations, you've done the impossible. You've worked up excitement in that universal paragon of apathy: a too-cool-for-school teenager.

Hell, forget school. Bozey was too cool to express enthusiasm about anything that wasn't a Kurt Cobain throwback or cutting-edge tech. Bozey was the last to arrive at parties, shaking his long hair out of his eyes and deigning to sip on a beer. Bozey was—oh shit! Bozey was waiting for me to reply.

'S-sounds nice. He sounds nice, I mean. I think. Like, I don't know. Um. What was he wearing?'

Polo stopped scratching Roger Fedora behind the ears for a minute to scrunch his nose at me. 'You're weird.'

Bozey hit Polo in the face with the cushion I'd chucked at him.

'Ow! What'd you do that for? Listen, let's roll.'

'Why? Hey, Tars, when do you go back to the States?'

'Less than two weeks, but I have to go to Delhi firs—'

'Because I have to kick your team's ass? Let's go to my room and FIFA it up, dude.'

Bozey hung back as Polo left the room. 'You coming, Tars?'

I laughed. 'Yeah, totally! I can never ever get enough of video games! Idiot.'

He grinned. 'So, like, do you want to go check out the new Italian place in Forum before you leave—'

'BOZEY!'

'COMING!'

'COME NOW!'

'COMING!'

'DUDE, FIFA'S SET UP!'
'COMING!'
'Oh my God, just go. You guys are giving me a headache.'
Looking frustrated, Bozey shuffled away and I scurried
online to see if I could find pictures of Jay giving the speech.

———

Under the golden glow of lights, so ostentatious that they
highlighted what they were supposed to hide (ill-executed Dilli
*shoshagiri*. At least they complemented the splurged-on Fendi
purse spilling lipstick and crumpled cash by Nitwit's feet), in
a living room thick with glass platters and kebabs and mint
sauce and gossiping aunts and stocks-are-up, pour-the-Walker
uncles, I sent Polo a text:

Get me out of here.

He texted me back from Calcutta:

Thank God for my exams. Just eat and ignore.

A large chunk of family had gathered for dinner the day
before Nitwit's engagement at my uncle's house. My cousins,
Nitwit and Tania, and their dozens of giggling girlfriends are
the ubiquitous south-Delhi babes, designer-decked empty
drums, asses covered in unicorn hair. I couldn't bear to be around
them; my skin grew uncomfortable and clunky.

It wasn't that they were ever anything less than distractedly
nice to me. But I had never been thin enough to pass muster
as not-fat, committed the incessant sacrilege of not sporting
a very specific version of beauty, and didn't have a boyfriend
whom I was trying to nudge towards marriage. It made me as
inscrutable to them as they were to me. And I was just politely
dismissed, perhaps as a failure.

I wore a heavy armour of America around Delhi, combat boots and Genette books. In my head I was still topping off my Parliament with a dash of coke and laughing about the narrative structure of Ke$ha's life with Asher.

And under it all, I found it incredibly unfair that they were so validated in their own eyes that the universe seemed to recognize it and reward them in kind, giving them the only riches they desired. They always seemed so happy to me, and what was that all about?

———

Tania walked into her bedroom with a friend, where I sat dressed for the engagement party, reading an Augusten Burroughs e-book on my laptop.

They looked me over, taking in the black silk sari I'd borrowed for the occasion and the old gold jewellery Aunty Agnes had left behind. My mother had offered me fashionable lehengas and polki-crusted necklaces, of course. Offered, to the point of insisting. But this old gold was all that Aunty Agnes had left of herself. This, and the birds. Except that The Wolf had opened up the hatch on their cage after she had been buried and they had flown away, every last one of them.

She had been a whole person, and this was all that remained, and I couldn't let this little bit fade away in the dark hollows of a forgotten locker.

Tania's friend spoke up, genuine concern lacing her words, 'Baby, are you going to go like this only?'

'I mean, I'll brush my hair first.'

'But that sari is *black*, no. It's bad luck!'

Tania was peering in the mirror, scrutinizing the mask of make-up on her face. 'Baby, just let her wear it. It's slimming na, at least.'

---

Tara: Ash, I can't fucking be here anymore . . .

Asher: Why not?

Tara: These people are insane. They're fucking aliens. Like, I might just lose my mind if I have to stay here much longer.

Asher: Oh God, just drink.

Tara: I'm trying! But there are people around all the time. Family and servants and stuff.

Asher: That sounds horrible.

Tara: It is.

Asher: Ugh.

Tara: Listen, I'm going to say school's starting a week early and stop by Amsterdam before going back. It's the only way I'm getting out of Delhi. You should come join me.

Asher: Damn. I've always wanted to go to Amsterdam.

Tara: Hahaha. So bad, it's good.

Asher: Hm. How expensive is it going to be?
Tara: Not that much. Couple Ks.

Asher: Ugh. I can't.

Tara: Asherrrr. I don't want to go alone ⊗

Asher: You'll totally die if you go alone.

Tara: Right. So seeing that we have that ascertained— come with me?

Asher: I don't have the money, Tara ⊗

Tara: ⊗

Asher: You know I would if I could. I'm way past my credit limit already ⊗

Tara: Can't you just apply for another card?

Asher: I mean, I guess I could . . .

Tara: And that would give you enough to buy a ticket and stuff, right? We can always figure the rest out!

Asher: You are a horrible influence upon my life.

Tara: Oh come on, you're a product of America. It's basically your duty to do this.

Asher: FINE!

Tara: Yessss! I love you ☺

Asher: You're a manipulative bitch.

Tara: Haha! Well, we only live once. Tick-tock, baby girl—let's go!

———

We are here. We arrived at some neon-lit night, all blue waves and black lights. We have lips on our tongues and smoke in our lungs. The music beats pound bass, sex. We soak till we bleed dancing juice and drop to Tiësto and the Swedish House Mafia. We dance with our feet in the air, and nails, orange and pink and purple, trace lines on necks and burrow tighter in hair. When the morning comes, we fall into our darkened holes and sleep till it's time to repeat.

For tonight, they are my best friends, these girls and boys I'll never know. I'll hold his hand across the crowded bar and help her unzip her red bodysuit outside the smoky stalls in the restroom. I'll try not to look down the long length of her legs and hold myself back from brushing against the naked stretch of skin cut out of her backless dress. He'll guide me through the jostling crowd and right now, he is, she is, they are my best friends in the whole world.

I used to watch these people from an untouchable distance. These boys who look like the gods of my childhood, and the girls who drove them to drink and song by wearing their skirts too short and their hair too lovely.

So tonight, you'll be my best friends. And for the five hours we shine underneath strobe lights, I will give you the best damn time you've ever had. I'll look at you with a hopeless admiration, like you're the prettiest girl in the room, like I can't take my eyes off you. And when you reach for me—because you will—I'll never let you know that it's really only the me refracted through you that I can't stop staring at, never let you know that your whole world is only a necessary game to win.

Asher and I ran, danced, breathed, lived on alcohol and adrenaline. Claimed everything. Stretched our bodies because nobody wanted our souls. We blew lines and in and out of lives, and we had different best friends every night.

And the boy that I love, the only peace of salvation in the relentless anarchy of my world? I had to put him aside for a little while. I had to forget him, just a little, just for now

while

there was a room on a street in a house with a bed; I was looking out over the Amstel. What a pretty name for what a pretty river, I thought, standing by a window in the room on the street in the house with a soft bed tousled by sheets that smelled like a baby's head. What a pretty name, indeed, and what a fuckshit would I be to spoil the view with an errant, terrible blotch.

I wanted a cigarette. I had a cigarette. I asked him to have one too and he said he didn't smoke, so I asked him are you sure and he smiled and took it. He was cute when he smiled. The small dimple in his right cheek wiped some of the asshole off his face. I wondered why he took the cigarette.

Seven hours ago, in a hotel room with porn strung up as artwork, Asher and I had debated the consequences of snorting bad blow. Well, not bad, exactly. Contaminated. New York snow.

'The hell, Ash, didn't you check this before you paid?'

'I did. It looks so pretty!'

'Asher. There is glitter in this. Glitter!'

'I think it's leftovers off a hooker's belly.'

I tried to be pissed but the degree to which this was expected pretty much rendered that pointless. Ever since he'd burst out of the closet, Asher had been climbing a steady upswing of flamboyance. He'd gone from layered, collared prep to sequins before noon, and the only reason it was more amusing than irritating is that everything Asher does is ironic. Or is it? You can never tell. That's the fun part.

There was nothing to be done but snort the sparkling coke. And then, when we were outside, thank God—or whatever we believed in—that this was Amsterdam. Thank you, for not drawing censure to our brightened eyes and giving us places to put our heightened hearts.

We walked into slow-flying strobes and I felt an instinctive rush of fierce dislike as soon as I saw him. His neon-green muscle tee is so contrived. And he's wearing aviators. In a club. At night. Fucking douchebag.

Obviously, I made eye contact and drained my drink. Two stones, three birds, one douchebag in a fluorescent shirt.

He brought the equally obvious Absinthe over, said something in French or a really thick accent. It's too loud to hear him anyway.

The game is always the same; hadn't this guy's twin brought over *Jäger* yesterday? But who wants to think now. Thought is the enemy, thought is an infected wound, thought is a wedding card with your family name on it and cold hands, and then later, yes, relief. But thought is you, and I can't think about you. I can't think about you, but elementary, dear mess, that's all I ever do.

This is the music that reminds me of You, all these songs that Oakenfold and Tiësto and Benassi play. It is never in the Great Love Songs that I find you, never even in Marlow or Donne. I am surprised by this, but then, not altogether confused; the depths of my love will never be a sanguine calm. It will always be fire or nothing at all.

Maybe it's the way this music swells. This music that haunts our haunts, we who are somehow compelled by our youth to dance together in the dark. It crescendoes step by step, beat by beat, key by key, till it becomes round and fat and pregnant. And we feel unborn, we are just the dark shapes of embryos filled with possibility: there could be love, here, tonight. There could be forgiveness and validation and answers and retribution. But the darkness pounds like crazy and our poisons drive us to regrets and frenzy.

Regrets and frenzy. Regrets, and frenzy. It used to be stupidity, frenzy, then regret.

As suddenly, as unstoppably, as always, there is a short quick jab of memory, of something you said, something you didn't say. A short, quick jab of euphoria blanketed blue by melancholy. Something to look for again, something to find in different places with different people, something to create because really, it can never be found anywhere else.

Inside the euphoria without him, I chose lesser things. I chose that bed in that room, I left my dress on the stairs of that house, I turned my head into those sheets and they smelled like a baby's head.

Four years and five days have passed and I cannot forget him.

# *Flux Pavilion*

Time has this unfortunate habit of acting like a difficult child if you don't watch it carefully. It's been bad lately, running away when the babysitter's back was turned. Four years gone, and where did they go? The last snows on these roads that are veins etched into my consciousness, and where did it all go? We had so much time. Whole, fat years of it.

Nicole and I, laying on the grass beside Glass Lake, American sun fresh in my eyes. 'Don't ask me how I am, Ziggy. It's the most cruel of all pleasantries. When you ask someone how they are, you're just tempting the askee with a question social dictates don't allow them to answer. So don't ask me how I am, and stop trying to sell Tara your damn pot, okay?'

Asher growing out of his gangly closet. Asher drunk and trailing glitter down Main Street. Asher broken for a moment, on the floor, in the dark, asking me if it would always be like this.

Author—Implied Author—Narrator— NARRATIVE—
Narratee—Ideal Reader—Reader

And when the parts are laid bare, all the stories start to make sense.

David calling me free like a sad prophet—wrong, after all.

In the days before I must leave, I removed myself from my life. I stopped taking calls from friends, stopped going to One for karaoke and drinks. I sat hopelessly in classes all day and rode the campus buses in endless loops at night.

It's too much to let the end be the end. An end bears easier if it has already happened and you're left looking back—not living the breathless devastation inherent in a true moment of goodbye. So while it wasn't yet over, I looked back on what could not be, again, with doomed, dashed longing.

On the depth and texture of this life. The irretrievability of this time. On Asher, on Nicole, on drunk Jane, beautiful Jane, kissed-me-back-because-she-was-drunk Jane, sad Jane, we-jumped-in-the-lake Jane. We thawed off in the shower, we pulled in David: ménage a *faux*.

———

'In Soviet Sandvitch Shop, you don't make sandvitch, sandvitch is made for you.'

What?

'What?'

'In Soviet Sandvitch Shop, you don't make—'

'No, I heard you. I just don't—What?'

He laughed. 'It's three in the morning and I'm in here alone. I have to entertain myself somehow, right?'

Relieved, but also pissed at myself for not being cool enough to catch on and play along, I quirked a half-smile, then felt like a bitch and laughed too hard.

'Right. Can I get the number four?'

'Sure. You have really pretty eyes, by the way.'

'Um, thanks. I'd like that toasted, please.'

It felt weird being so standoffish, because I could distinctly remember the feeling of being unfazed in the face of faze. But I hadn't talked to anyone in days and my voice felt rusty from lack of use.

It occurred to me that I was subconsciously preparing to return home. Ha. Home, did I just think? Where is home, Tara? No—don't panic. Just breathe. Stop. It's okay. Figure it out. You still have some time. Figure out what home is.

'Do you want any dressing on this? I could even make some just for you.'

'Wha—ew!'

He laughed. It was a good-humoured laugh, cleaning up his entendre.

'No, no dressing. This is good, thanks.'

He sliced tomatoes on to five-grain bread, lay down a line of black olives, wrapped it in a blanket of basil and sprinkled oregano over the whole thing. As I watched him, I saw his face not in the brightly lit sandwich shop, but somewhere else, somewhere I couldn't quite place.

'Hey, where do I know you from?'

'Now you're just making it too easy.'

I laughed. 'No, really, I feel like we've met before.'

'Have we? I feel like I'd have remembered meeting you.'

'Mm, it's not coming to me right now, but I'm pretty sure we have, yeah.'

'So, I get off work in an hour. How do you feel about getting a coffee with me?'

'Ah, I'm sorry, I have an insane amount of work to get done this week.'

'Ouch. Okay, here you go. On the house.' He handed me the wrapped sandwich.

'Oh no, please don't!'

'It's done, pretty lady. Think of it as a reward for being a good person.'

'How do you know I'm a good person?'

'Aren't you?'

'Nope. I eat babies.'

'Fried?'

'Baked. One tries to be healthy.'

He started cracking up and I asked whether they had a restroom before the repartee got away from me.

'Straight through there and to the left.'

'Thanks.'

In the bathroom, I paced for a while, working something off, some energy that was on edge. It worked, so I pulled out a torn scrap of tissue paper from my purse and scribbled a note in handwriting wrought barely legible by four years of typing college papers.

614632364

Call me so I can hear that crazy Russian accent again.
    —Tara

I put on some red lipstick like gunpowder, and slapped the tissue on to the counter as I walked out of the store. He looked up, surprised, but by the time he got to it, I had left the door swinging behind me.

It felt like a sufficiently badass thing to do. I plugged Flux
Pavilion into my ears and walked fast. Angled my head down
like a hat on *Mad Men*. Like a cocky hat on a man on *Mad
Men*; Caucasian and American. Red lips dangled a white
cigarette on to a blue flame, and I walked away to the growing,
unconcerned beats.

# The Towers of Perth

**6145678289:** Hi there ☺ Will I be shot down again if I ask you to dinner tomorrow night?

**Tara:** Russian accent guy?

**6145678289:** Yes, ma'am.

**Tara:** I think I remembered where I know you from.

**Russian Accent Guy:** Let's hear it!

**Tara:** Well if I'm wrong this is going to sound really weird, but did you go to this weird Halloween party at River Rapids Park

**Russian Accent Guy:** Oh no, that's an affirmative. Did I do something bad?

**Tara:** Haha, nope. You just sold me some pills.

**Russian Accent Guy:** That would have been the army-issued stuff, so I hope it was at least good?

**Tara:** It definitely was. How long were you in the army?

**Russian Accent Guy:** A little under two years, before I got a medical discharge. So is it a yay or nay on dinner tomorrow?

**Tara:** I'm going to go with the former ☺ 7 p.m. work for you?

**Russian Accent Guy:** Could you give me till 7.30? I'm teaching this self-defence class that doesn't get out till 6.30, and I need a little time to go home and sexify after that.

**Tara:** Haha, by all means, take your time to sexify. 7.30 it is. What kind of self-defence?

**Russian Accent Guy:** It's a mix of ju-jitsu and some other forms that the government calls 'combatives'. And great, it's a date. Address?

**Tara:** 100 Macarrow Street, Apt D. Right off Main past Eighth. And wow, that sounds pretty cool. Question—have you ever killed anyone?

**Russian Accent Guy:** Lol. Not directly.

**Tara:** How do you kill someone indirectly?

**Russian Accent Guy:** I was a human intelligence collector/interrogator.

**Tara:** That sounds absolutely TERRIFYING. I'm getting mental images of Hannibal Lecter slicing bits off that guy's brain and cooking it before feeding it to him.

**Russian Accent Guy:** Lol, torture is illegal. Words were my battlefield. I just convinced people they should tell me what they knew. And the information I provided led to the deaths of several people. Although I didn't pull the trigger and the information possibly saved lots of innocent people and all that, I still feel guilty.

**Tara:** What happened to make us so insensate, as a race?

**Russian Accent Guy:** The absence of a God.

**Tara:** You don't think there's a God?

**Russian Accent Guy:** There are gods, yes. Just not any that are ours, the human race's.

**Tara:** Hm. Well I'd have to disagree with you on that front. But this is a long disagreement to have over a protracted dinner, and I should really turn in now if I'm going to be productive in the least tomorrow.

**Russian Accent Guy:** All right, lady. I'm excited about our date. Sleep well.

**Tara:** Thanks, you too. And as a parting diatribe—I HATE sleep. As a concept, I mean. It's such a waste of time. The only time it would be useful as a voluntary device would be to block out the world when having a rough day or something. Though actually, ice cream can take care of that too.

**Russian Accent Guy:** Aw, what about dreams?

*Pour a little salt, we were never here*

—Bon Iver, 'Skinny Love'

# Good Winter

I never stopped riding the buses. Around and around, around in circles. I rode till I ran out of thoughts. Till I fell asleep, till the part of my head that hurt from laying on the cold pane poked me awake. It was dark, by then, and cold. Always cold. Always snow and soaked boots, because it was dark and it was cold and I couldn't see where I was going.

When the buses stopped running, when the driver squinted at me through the dividing glass because even he had noticed me amongst the endless streams of people getting on and off, and he didn't know why I had been sitting there for six hours but he wanted me to leave because he and the bus were done for the night, then I had to step off my rolling friend. Sometimes he had to wake me up and I could tell that it made him very uncomfortable.

Once I was off the bus, being anywhere felt too stationary, the still air too suffocating. So I walked around, making paths, taking circuitous routes that skirted a return home. One day, I did not stop walking. I had dreamt of wolves that night. I had dreamt they were baying (I could assume for blood, but I could be assuming wrong. This was, after all, a very strange dream) and I was inside a small house made of logs; I was inside, where I had lit a fire for warmth and light, and they were outside, in the cold and dark and snow. Baying.

I know this was a dream because I do not know how to build a fire.

I didn't stop walking because I had had that dream, and I was not sure when I had woken up. And I kept walking.

I walked on the bridge. It wasn't a bridge that allowed pedestrians but it was very late and very dark and very cold and no one was out to see. The bridge unfurled ahead of me and behind me, largedarkhulk. Its towers had masks on them, imperturbable faces of glinting steel. Some professors called it the Neo-Fascist bridge and said the university had built it to be grand, to impress or intimidate anyone entering this sprawling campus reigning in the heart of this city.

I liked this idea. I like grand structures and big human-made things that sprint towards the sky and spread across acres of land. They make me feel safe, provide proof that I belong to a commune that can build things to last.

I walked off the bridge, I walked to the riverbank, and it looked to me, though I could not be certain, that the frozen surface was bloodied at the edges, bleeding on to the banks.

There was a bigroundmoon in the sky.

It shone very bright.

There was endless more sky around it.

*At once I knew, I was not magnificent*

The cold fell in waves from above. There were folds of cold in the air. I put my tongue out and it tasted like that bad kind of sweet, like the aftertaste of a diet Coke.

I walked to the only lights, to the small house made of logs.

Inside, the place looked like a small house made of logs should. He was sitting on the floor, writing on a square scrap of paper that he'd balanced on the ball of his knee.

I took off my scarf and I took off my coat. I made myself at home.

'There's aspartame in the air.'

'Come sit.'

I did.

Patient silence as he wrote.

'Would you pass me that baggie next to you?'

I passed him the baggie.

He pulled the leaves apart like they mattered.

He mixed them with brown tobacco and thickly sprinkled the mixture into the square scrap of poetry.

I licked the edges and felt the melting line of bitter blue ink on my tongue.

He struck a match and I took a breath.

Patient silence as I smoked.

Patient silence as he smoked.

'I walked into a cliff once. Right through it. And I came out on the other side, a little wet and a little blue, but there were miles, miles, miles of rock faces that rose into the skies, a sea of land, swept clean by virgin air.'

'Where?'

'Milwaukee.'

Patient silence as we smoked.

'What happened to you?'

'I was left for broken.'

'And?'

'And I was.'

It seemed to me, in that moment, that all I had ever wanted was to touch him, to feel the actuality of his flesh, realize the reality of his existence, to know, to know, to know he lived and he was.

I knew that this was not true. That is not all I had ever wanted. I could distinctly remember—only one thing because it was hard to engage in the busy task of concrete recollection—but I could remember that one particular strong, strong want: when I would walk through the mall and smell the fresh-baked cookies and want a brandy snap so badly that I could just about feel the crack of biscuit and the ooze of cream.

So I knew what seemed to me then, that all I had ever wanted was to touch him, to feel the actuality of his flesh, to know—I knew that was a lie. But right then I could not deny the feeling. Right then, in the infinite universe suspended in that infinitesimal moment, it was my truth.

'Did you rebuild yourself?'

'How could I?'

'Redemption? Acceptance? Moving on? Forgetting?'

He almost laughed.

'No, I just stilled my soul.'

'God?'

'Earth and us.'

'Earth and us?'

He walked over to me. He walked against the firelight; his silhouette was lit up.

And I thought he was going to kiss me, but I only thought that because I was too literal, too not enough of a person. I am ashamed of how little I was when he came and stood behind me. In the firelight, he traced the line of my arm, traced a line along deep blue crepe.

'This is a pretty blouse.'

I am a little person and I think he will kiss me.

He whispered in my ear, called me a name I am not.

'Not on the mouth, my dear, not on your lips. Not on you.'

And he whisper-sings a song into my ear, and it is the most beautiful collection of sentiments masquerading as sounds that I have ever heard. I am stripped of flesh and bone in its wake, overwhelmed by the sheer force of its beauty.

'You are magnificent.'

'I'm just snow.'

'And you have left invisible stains in this world.'

'And we have left invisible stains on the world.'

'In mine, in my world, you have been a havoc, all the change.'

He tipped his head in acknowledgement then. I think he might even have smiled a little.

'You are very sad always, are you not?'

'I don't know why.'

'I like to think to be one person is too little for you.'

I looked at him some more. In the end, we do what we have to.

'You have to go now.'

'I do.'

And I could only feel a tight finality in my chest, the complete and utter absence of an alternate ending. The world would be just that—just the world.

I said it again, to tell myself. 'I do. And you?'

'I'll be here.'

So I left, but I sang a little as I did so. Boots soaked in cold and snow, lined white with the salted sidewalk, lined light with a song.

*Cut out all the ropes and let me fall*

It hadn't really happened at all.

                              It was all just a dream.

But I know it happened.

                        What can anyone     know, really?

                            e

                            v

                              e

                                 r

                    and I am here now,

                and it is over     it is hot and dusty

It happened. It happened                and I am here now.

# Twenty Pounds of Flesh

**Books**

**Style Over Matter, and What Could Have Been**

*By P.Rossett*

*Published: 28 July 2013*

*Tara Mullick obviously wants her first novel to debut with a bang. Mullick and her publishers have pulled out all the stops to ensure that* Frequencies *creates a strong buzz with its arrival. The requisite 'groundbreaking' and 'this is a seminal representation of our times' sound bites have been garnered and shouted about by PR personnel, and Mullick herself sold as a bright new star in the world of pretentious pop fiction.*

*So what's all the fuss about?*

*In* Frequencies, *Mullick loosely traces the process of her self-imposed conformation to American culture and the subsequent sense of detachment from her own roots. She goes from leading a sheltered, joint-family life in Kolkata to drinking and doing drugs while at college in America. It is not a new story, but she filters it via an emphasis on run-of-the-mill existentialism and a foggy relationship with a globe-trotting billionaire whose affectations she idolizes. Mullick relegates the postcolonial aspect of her story to the background, keeping her protagonist focused outside the shifting cultural scenery around her. In effect, the treatment of immigration back and forth as a foregone, comfortable conclusion for the affluent youth of a New India says more about the world she lives in than the novel itself.*

*It has to be said that at least Mullick is a ballsy writer. Relentlessly self-referential, this postmodern pastiche of all that is popular highlights her Generation Z sensibility in spades, lathering the book with an endless array of allusions ranging from Virginia Woolf to The Killers to Bon Iver (the latter's Justin Vernon features briefly as a dreamlike character of sorts). Think a literary version of the pop culture-heavy music of Lady Gaga, and you get an idea of the overtly declarative, yet frequently vacuous, nature of Mullick's style.*

*The biggest flaw of* Frequencies—*and this is a deeply flawed novel—is that it tries to do too much, in too many ways, and ends up barely grazing the surface of any of the myriad issues Mullick addresses. Pontifications on everything from bar-hopping to sex to life itself, and flirtations with religion and the communist politics of West Bengal are just that—minor flirtations that flit by without ever delving into the meat of any matter.*

*In a display of egregious overconfidence, Mullick makes her plot skip around spatially and temporally till the reader is left feeling disjointed and confused. The story itself is sparse, bereft of detail and coherent arcs, and the protagonist—an obvious extension of Mullick herself—is self-involved to the point of being loathsome. She indulges in herself and her flights of frenzy like an absolute hedon, with barely enough cause to justify any of her self-destructive tendencies.*

Mullick's twenty-two years are reflected, mostly for the worse, in her writing. Apart from a surprisingly beautiful epilogue wherein she exercises precision and restraint to deliver a bleak ending, her language is ostentatiously, unnecessarily over-decorated, failing to lend her story the cohesiveness it needed. That might not have been altogether amiss had Mullick's voice been more defined. As it stands, however, Frequencies is chock-full of experimental writing done in a shaky voice, more reminiscent of Creative Writing 500 than the feel of polished avant-garde that she seems to be going for.

In a word, Frequencies is gimmicky. Fortunately for Mullick, some of those gimmicks are catchy enough to induce a chuckle or two. The tag cloud she uses as a back-cover summary is somewhat innovative, as is her cheeky inclusion of a self-penned book review interwoven into the narrative. The constant barrage of intertextuality, random detours into poetry and second person, and over-formatted structural styling, though, are trite and more reflective of mediocre blogger culture than the literary weight that Mullick unsuccessfully tries to lend to them.

All in all, this first novel left me with a sense of what could have been. If Mullick had concentrated on the interesting arc of her uniquely placed postcolonial ponderings or on building a more compelling story, the end result might have been eminently readable. Instead, we are left with the appetizer of potential, waiting hungrily for an entrée that never arrives.

----

The second floor patio outside L'Opera lay open underneath
a cold winter sky, bathed by Delhi's perennially hot sun.
I brought out a cheery slice of mille-feuille and a coffee from
the patisserie and settled into a wrought-iron chair, waiting for
the caffeine and cream to kick-start a temporary alleviation of
my black mood.

Two tables away, the only other person haunting the patio
in the middle of a working Tuesday lingered over a litter of
espresso cups. White hair, cream chiffon, double-strand seed
pearls; a Yash Chopra heroine gone grey,

*Had Jay and I met inside fading bodies*

ashing her cigarette into the wind; long, slim ones from a
light blue box—

*closer to ash than flesh at eighty-three*

Vogues. I'd only ever seen them in Europe—the long,
slim fingers of a Polish hooker draped around them, offering
me one, two, the whole box diffusing through us by the
Amstel.

*lost,*

She was

*instantly, irrevocably;*

blowing out precisely curled plumes, stylized to perfection
like the rest of her. Polished, gimmicky and overtly declarative.

*discarded time and irrelevant space.*

I didn't know what to do next. Everyone I knew was working
towards something, some sort of goal—a job, a better job,
marriage, kids, something. And I, unable to commit anywhere,
unable to belong to anything, stood immobile, rooted to
indecision.

It occurred to me that I was my only claimant. I belonged only to myself, to the things that bound me into consciousness. The rest was just noise.

Jay had been my only constancy, the shape of that love the only immortal thing within me. And I had poured all of it into *Frequencies* over the past four years. I had kept myself preoccupied for these past few months after coming back to India for good and moved to Jay's city, meeting publishers and working on turning my leaden pile of prose into something they would put on store shelves.

But it was done now. The book was out, the reviews had said what they had to say, and I supposed the most emotionally profitable thing to do was to chalk the damn thing down to some sort of success.

I was living alone for the first time, in a large, airy apartment that belonged to a distant aunt, and did a good job of keeping up the deception of independence. Not that I really cared. My brother had started school in California, and Button and Cookie were both interning across Europe, so it wasn't like I had anywhere to go, nor had I, in my protected, bubble-bound school years, made any unsavoury friends whom I could now bring back home. India was stifling, infected with an incredible social striation that turned cities teeming with millions into villages. There was nothing I could do without having to consider a hundred variables first, mentally tracing routes back and forth, walking in and out of Zara when I really just wanted to slide into a bar.

In desperate times, the couple of cousins I had in the city were my desperate measure. One of them was getting married. It appeared to be their news of the century.

Resolved to be a good sport, I volunteered to accompany Nitwit on a fitting for her bridal lehenga, a dazzling spectacle that could, in the event of a power failure, light up the wedding venue as an added benefit.

In the car, en route to the fitting, she talked small to me.

'How was America, Taru baby?'

You wouldn't understand the half of it. 'Good.'

'You were there for so long, na? What were you doing?'

Earning a degree and smoking pot. 'Getting a degree.'

'Did you have to study a lot and all?'

No. I'm smart. 'Yeah, a little. It's not that bad.'

Nits threw open long eyelashes. 'But it must be hard, na?'

I shrugged, suddenly angry, wanting to spit spite, to tell her that this, this trying to talk to her doe eyes and dull brain, was much, much harder.

'Did you do Honours?'

'We have majors. Mine were Narrative Theory and pre-law.'

Suddenly, she perked up. 'You're a lawyer?'

Jesus.

'No, I'm just qualified to go to law school if I choose to do so. I took courses that are like prep for the LSAT. Liberal Arts stuff.'

I had lost her attention midway through the sentences, but for some perverse, panicked reason, felt the need to reclaim it. 'But I did study the law a little, yes.'

'Accha, so tell me something. How long do I have to stay married to Jigar?'

'Huh?'

'How long?'

'What?'

'*Arre*, how long till he owes me half the money?'

'What—Nits, what? What are you—why are you marrying this guy?'

'I have to, baby. I'm almost twenty-seven, na.'

———

I voiced incredulousness to her sister.

'We all hope for a happy marriage, Taru. But girls have to be careful.'

'Neha, it's unethical in the extreme, what she's doing!'

'Just be happy for your sister, okay.'

She isn't my sister. She is my mother's brother's second-eldest daughter, but I call her my sister. Because we do that in India. We do that especially in Delhi. Falsely inflate the value of relationships, ascribe love to predetermined bonds. We do this because blood is important; we wear its stains like a badge. We take pride in the good and consider it our benevolent duty as kin to fix the bad.

Me, I was as bad as they came. I looked all wrong. Wore combat boots and ripped shirts with Marley or Cobain on them. Read too much and couldn't tell a tube of mascara from a marker pen. I talked about the wrong things and didn't know how to flirt without making it obvious that I was doing it, without putting sex on the table. That, I found out, is the key trick for survival in south Delhi. Tricking the boys into wanting you, making a career out of denying your body so that his can be addled into marrying you before he even realizes what's happened.

Not that he minds, of course. Ownership has its own rush.

I spent a while acclimatizing, registering but not comprehending, bombarded by words that didn't quite make sense in relation to each other, until they did.

'Baby, what's happened to your skin? Why've you become so tanned?'

'Taru, lose some weight na. You've got such a pretty face.'

All my hard-won American cool didn't seem worth quite as much in the face of their absolute conviction that their lives were valid, were right, and slowly the venom soaked through. First, I was confused and then I was shocked and then I was concerned, and then, then I was acutely self-conscious. It is important to be beautiful, I learned. That lesson had somehow escaped me in the foggy foliage of Narnia, slipped my grasp along the cold alleys and corridors of my campus. But it started to show itself now, and again, I think: Do beautiful people know the tremendous possibility of their lives? Do they know that, at any given point of time, there is the possibility that someone is regarding them a revelation? Someone is watching the curves of their bones, feeling the relentless pull of the very way they are arranged.

Still, I feel a terrible longing (because that is all jealousy is, really) to be this, this thing we call beauty that lies under everything great that has ever been done. Every great monument, every timeless song, every blustering kid building resolve at the shining head of hair blocking his view of the blackboard.

Oh of course, I know—that old argument. It's love, not beauty. Beauty lies in the loving eyes of the beholder. Yes, fine, all right. But where does love begin? That fire-riddled kind of love, I mean, not the slow burn of something that grows out of time and familiarity and necessity and age. The kind of love, in short, that writes songs and builds immortal white marble tombs—let's call it passion; let's, only for now, as a placeholder, give it that dirty little label. That strain of love (and there are those who would call it the only kind worth having) is rooted in beauty. It is rooted in the inspiration that comes from something that sets your breath on fire. It comes from feeling felled to your knees, cut off at the crease, because it is built like worship, looking up at something that high—at her beauty and his, at the relentless pull of the very way they are arranged. You have to do something, you have to get it out, you have to let them know, you have to.

It's not even hard to do, because when you open the page, the words that come out are always about him. And when you touch the piano, her eyes dance across the keys that must become the notes to your song.

Sometimes I think I would do the proverbial things you think you wouldn't, all for something as proverbially silly (is it?) as beauty. Like kill; push a red button, slice a blue vein. Because I want so much to feel that skein of breathless possibility shimmer over my spotless skin. Because no one I know ever wrote a song for an unsightly face.

They say it's ephemeral, that's the argument against it. Beauty is fleeting, character lasts forever. Or some variation of that. And it's true, it will die. But it will have been, and an end is nothing in the face of what has been.

Besides, life is ephemeral, and that's the ultimate democratic gift. Everyone who is has life. Why don't we all get to be beautiful?

(And the answer to this is the whispered truth they don't tell us; that it isn't free—it isn't luck or destiny that has brought you this, these perfect lines and fathoms-deep eyes. Somehow, somewhere along the way, you have paid the price and you have killed, killed, killed. You have been borne by oppressors and murderers and the daughters of oppressors and murderers, or you have broken someone, or you have taken something. It doesn't come for free. You pay for it. If there is beauty on your face, there has been blood on your hands.)

———

As my beliefs floundered, as my thoughts grew mired in flux, I found an anchor in the numbers all around.

I counted. I counted ceaselessly. I counted my steps when I climbed the stairs, and I felt fear on the third step and the thirteenth step. I thought of good things on the fourth step and the seventh step. I counted the laps I swam and the bites I ate, and you would think it was about the calories but it's not, it's not. It's about keeping the numbers right, keeping the butterfly's wings from flapping wrong, a desperate attempt to maintain a balance I know I cannot, but that I also know I must. Numbers, counting, balance, trying.

———

I was bad today and I ate a banana. Carbs.
The little pills that make me thin
And sometimes I think, what have I become?

————

Every day, I go for a run. Where once I rode the buses, now I run. I run because, well, there aren't any quiet buses in India. None where you can just sit and be left alone, left alone to be. No, there's shoving and filth and men with dirty eyes. There's *excoose-pliz, pliz-medam, ektu-adjust.* And too many bodies. Pressed up, pushed in, packed. Packed like sardines.

But I also run because I can't sit still anymore. I cannot let the weight of my thoughts settle into me. I cannot stop, cannot let the thoughts catch up. I count.

I run and I count, I count and I run.

As I run, the flesh falls off my bones. Everything extra is burned away.

Spare, dense. Bones. Remember?

Unembellished, honest. Lighter, heavy.

I feel the change more than I see it. I sense the small shifts in fate with the sloughing of fat. In the mirror, I still see the bump on a nose, the flappy-ness of an earlobe and hair that grows too fast. But I feel the turn of heads and the lingering of looks. I accept fresh deference with barely concealed disdain, but I can't say I don't want it.

I get a measure of beauty and I pay for it with a measure of tragedy—lost, the irretrievable ability to use my body to my fill, to be okay with the fact that it is dying.

(And I think maybe the answer had it all wrong. Maybe the whispered truth was just a disguised lie. That, yes, it certainly isn't free, it isn't luck or destiny that has brought you this, these perfect lines and fathoms-deep eyes. Somehow, somewhere along the way, you have paid the price and you have been killed, maimed, killed. You have been broken by someone and you have had something taken from you. It doesn't come for free. You pay for it. If there is beauty on your face, there has been blood in your hands.)

———

I looked at the picture and I could feel the walls. Pitted, like pockmarked skin, like smooth but pockmarked skin, the face of the walls. The carpets below were synthetic, scratchy. And it was always cold because it was always 5 a.m. and we had just started actually getting some studying done an hour ago. The cold pizzas and cold cookies lay strewn between the laptops and cords and Chipotle cups and notebooks. Not too many text books because it was a state school and most people were too poor or too cheap to buy them.

I looked at the picture and I could feel the concrete beneath my feet. I could feel the grass off to the side. The weight of the buildings that sat solidly around. The walk to class, the walk to biddable Austen and forbidden Rushdie, to magical Borges and inscrutable Joyce. The walk to chicken salad sandwich and Cherry pop at lunch, then a sizzling cigarette in the cold wind. The walk back home, away from biddable Austen and forbidden Rushdie, away from magical Borges and valiantly trying to scrute Joyce.

I looked at Nicole and fairies lit up a line down my face.

I looked at it all, and I remembered it all, and I knew, I knew I could never forget any of it. What I perhaps did not know was that there is a fine line, a silver-spun tightrope, between not forgetting and not being able to let go. A Gatsby baby, after all, beating against the current as though the inevitable had come as a surprise.

I made the collage of pictures my computer wallpaper and I looked at it for hours. I looked at it and ate the chicken salad sandwich and drank the Cherry pop that I bought from the imported foods section at the fancy grocery store in the mall. I left the computer on as I went to bed and used the picture as my nightlight.

———

I think I missed Asher most of all.

He was all the me I had found in that world, all the me that made absolutely no sense here, in this one.

Asher always had the best taste in music of anyone I knew. He was incredibly obnoxious about it, though, and bluntly shamed people—even random strangers in the dorm lobby—listening to something off the Top 40. It pissed off most of our friends. I found it hilarious.

Sometime early in the spring of freshman year, I had dropped my phone on the sidewalk and cracked it broken. Asher had just changed over to the newly launched iPhone and let me have the spare he had lying around. There was an 8 GB memory card full of music wedged in it, and I found

The Shins and Shiny Toy Guns, Jack's Mannequin and Jimmy Eat World, Damien Rice and Greg Laswell's haunting take on Cindy Lauper. It became my most prized possession. I never asked him whether he'd left it in there on purpose or just forgotten to take it out.

We had always been close, but for the first few months after Nicole left, we were inseparable. Even now, we were still bound by the deepest ties of friendship—a shared past, the same humour, genuine affection and a doppelgänger understanding. But we had gathered others and turned into a group. For that period though, it was just the two of us. And this was probably because of the kind of things we liked to do.

I had just started smoking seriously, and was tutoring a coughing Asher into the habit. We found that cheap wine helped the smoke go down smoother. So there we were, drunk, walking down High Street, down a bottle each, sucking on minty Marlboro Menthols.

'What are we going to do?'

What, indeed?

Asher wasn't asking me for suggestions for what to do right then, of course. No, this was just the same question we asked each other every day, after we got drunk enough.

We never came up with any answers, obviously. We just tried to figure something out of the question, maybe locate a direction or throw some light on what lay ahead. It was when I tried to imagine a distant future—a life ten, twenty years down—that I started feeling like I was going to throw up. Maybe it was too much wine, or maybe I was just restless and fidgety and too alive for my own good.

'I think we're too alive for our own good.'

'Probably. We should go down to the shady part of town, where the shootouts happen.'

'Let's.'

'Are you serious?'

'Totally.'

'I was fucking kidding, Tara.'

I took a long, deep drag of the cigarette and it didn't burn enough. It wasn't killing me fast enough. It wasn't doing anything at all. Nothing was.

I exhaled as slowly as I could and looked him straight in the eye. 'Asher. We are too alive for our own good.'

It was like we'd timed it to a countdown. Three, two, one, and both of us took off, running along the busy street, shouting 'WE ARE TOO ALIVE!' into the wind. People scattered out a path for us until we ducked into one of the little alleys that bifurcated into more alleys, and then deep into the heart of Where The Shootouts Happen.

We stopped running then. The white kid from suburbia and the girl who grew up in a bubble in India felt very much like what they were. There weren't any people shooting or anything. Actually, there weren't any people around, period. But just the fact of the place was enough to scare us. We situated ourselves behind a dumpster.

'Ash AshAshAsh I'm scared I'm scared I'm scared I'm scare-'

'Shh, Tara, shut up!'

'Don't hiss at me!'

'Be quiet, then!'

'I'm tryin—'

There was a loud crash and clatter next to us. Asher froze.

I screamed. A skinny black cat stared disdainfully down from atop the dumpster.

'Fuck.'

I laughed. 'Yeah.'

Emboldened by our moment of jump-the-gun panic and feeling a little less alive, we executed a careful exploration of the area. We came across a crumbling house with a 'Condemned' sign on it. Asher said that it was clearly abandoned. We looked at each other and went in. Inside, it was very dark and very dusty. We followed the creaking staircase up to hollow bedrooms moonlit by bare windows. My skin prickled the way it used to on Caroline's beach, and I knew there were lonely ghosts blowing around this place too.

'Hey, Ash, let's see if we can go up any further.'

We could. A few more stairs later, we were upon a covered rooftop patio that looked up to downtown spreading over the sky.

It was abandoned, like the rest of the house. Left behind because it was unstable. But the view was incredible and the breeze, just the right shade of slight.

I felt the fiercest desire to be right where I was. I wanted to plant my feet into that ground, into this beautiful, abandoned, broken place and never leave it behind.

Looking over at Asher, I could see that he was experiencing the same kind of wonder at peace. Right then, right there, questioning the purpose of our existence did not seem all that important. It was a great feeling.

Over the next couple of nights, we returned and stashed piles of boxed wine and bottles of green-apple vodka on the roof, and proprietarily threw a blanket over the lot. For a few weeks, until we'd worked our way through the alcohol stash, it became our favourite place to hang out. We would look out over the city until liquor turned the lights hazy, and then lie down next to each other and sing along to The Shins or talk. On some nights—the best ones—we let the lyrics talk for us.

'Ash. You know how we always wonder what the point of life is?'

'Nothing?'

'Sometimes I think it might be nights like this.'

He nodded. Set up by the moment, we kissed. Something was off. I pulled away.

'Are you gay?'

He looked taken aback for a second, then shrugged. 'Yeah.'

I grinned at him. 'Thank God. That was a terrible kiss.'

'I know. It was SO bad!'

'Hey!'

'It sucked so much because I'm gay and you're a girl, right?'

'I think so?'

'It has to be!'

'There's no way we're that bad!'

'What if we actually are?'

'Oh my God, don't even say these things. I think we should practice, quickly.'

'Are you just trying to make out with me again?'

'Maybe just a little?'

We went through three boxes of wine that night. Shitty, but so good. And we kissed till we passed out on that abandoned roof. Platonic, but with tongue.

# The Brides

Nitwit makes a stunning bride. The groom is led in on a decorated, deafened horse amongst dancing pomp and spitting champagne. Parents look happy all around. Sold!

The last time I'd been to a wedding like this, I was seventeen and Jay had joined me at the water's edge. I looked around for him constantly, on the decent chance that Delhi's compressed high society might have brought him there. I didn't see him. But it was wedding season in his city, and he would be somewhere like this, somewhere where girls and silverware were glossed to a speckless shine, everything up for approval. It was all one big audition, and I wondered what he was making of it, whether he felt it run through him like an infection in his blood.

At four in the morning, the hour was deemed right; Neha and I were told to lead Nitwit to the mandap to begin the rites. Her fingers were frozen sticks and, in her eyes, I could see that she was seeing it all for the first time—the life stretching out before her, carpeted in Vuitton and hurdled in obligation.

It's the first time I actively feel the kinship that we were involuntarily born sharing. But it is too late now, Nitwit, it's far, far too late, and all I can do is hope to never be you. So

I swallow myself and tell her the only lie she wants to hear; I tell her not to worry, baby, it'll be okay. Then I hold her hand, walk her to the mandap, and watch as an orchid-strung noose is placed around her diamond-strung neck.

---

You will marry one of these girls, won't you? I'm sure she will be beautiful. Of course she will be. And she'll come from an old, grand family and be just right for you.

You will approve of the schools she went to, the lines of tennis apparent on her body. You will like her cultivation, talk yourself into being intrigued by her reservation. She will name the right authors and, because it has been so long since you played with fire, because you have mostly forgotten what that feels like, her studied intelligence will impress you. Enough. It will impress you just enough.

She will be a little concerned, of course. Your suit is faultless and your manners, impeccable. Your house has the right address and her parents look so very happy. But there's something just a little off about you, something she can't seem to put her finger on. Something amused in your eyes sometimes, and some small inattention, a moment where you drift into a world she can't quite see.

There is a kindness in you, and a practical wisdom that I loathe. You will want to make it work; you'll show her your world. Maybe not all of it, maybe not the part that is a savage animal hiding in Armani. You probably won't tell her, explicitly, how much you always want to win, that you need to win. That you need a life of constant battle because when you win, that's when you feel most alive. That is what vindicates the quiet, hidden hurts; the girl sipping a lying Bellini in Martha's Vineyard, the lovely morning newscaster on NBC who refused to want you.

But you won *her*, didn't you?

So you will get married. You will have an elegant wedding on a white January morning. The cold Delhi air will flap a wedding fire. People will eat hot cubes of sautéed tofu and smile and congratulate you. Old school friends will slap you on the arm and make jokes that you don't find funny anymore. College friends from the Upper East Side will look around interestedly, take anthropological stock. An ancient priest will tie an ancient knot. He will pull it tight, provide insurance to the union being formed. She will place her henna-adorned, gold-encrusted hands in yours. Her bangles will clink together. It will be the only sound, because it has gone quiet. The moment is here. It is about to happen. Everyone is waiting. The clinking will make you love her a little, in that moment, when she is bequeathing herself to you for life. It will remind you that she is a woman; the feminine tinkle will make you feel like a man. And then, the timeless, ageless chanting will begin. There will be vows. Promises. The merging of great families. A bond.

Maybe (and it could be that this is just me projecting hope) there will be a lightning instant of doubt as your hand, encasing hers, pours *samagri* into the fire. A short, quick fraction of a second where you feel an unexpected twinge that you can't quite explain. That will be me, my dearest; it will be me, somewhere, maybe even in the crowd—because you might invite me; we are friends, somewhat, after all—shattering inside a death knell.

But the samagri will be in the fire. It will be done. That will be that.

And your world will go on as it always has, never once aware of the wake of destruction those vows wrought on a girl who has loved you since she was seventeen, since she heard your voice on a fat old Nokia cell phone (that she never threw away; it had held your voice).

But I will have loved you. Know that. While you uncover her and she discovers you, while your mouth is on her wrist, moving up her arm and—no, no more. While that is happening, I will be trying to burn away every trace of you. I will drink something and smoke something and love someone. I will, I will try. But I will still have loved you. And somewhere in the atmosphere, some layer where the frequencies of our feelings are stored, there will be this: the memories of a voice making a seventeen-year-old head swim, of lazy eyes and admissions you didn't quite know you made. Of unbeknownst comfort given, and a racing pulse. Of the fiercest love I have ever felt, the strongest net you'll ever cast.

*December 2013*

# The Book Launch

Do you know the thing about frequencies, though? There's no denying them. You can call it chance, you can call it prayer, you can call it an author getting lazy and taking a shortcut. You can call it what you want, but dream all your dreams because if you push hard enough, even the universe will move.

———

With Nitwit married, I knew I was next in line. A few options had already been hinted at, random glowing recommendations of good boys making their way into conversations they had no business entering.

I couldn't say that the prospect didn't hold a momentary temptation. It was so easy, so convenient. It held the promise of an antiseptic kind of happiness, and you would have to be blind to not see that the prevalent opinion was that, reasonably speaking, it was more than anyone can ask for.

But what do you do when easy is invalidated in the face of something you've carried with you since you were seventeen?

What do you do with a feeling that lives its own grand, sovereign life? That sits there, irreverent and nonchalant, with an unshakeable hubris borne out of knowing that you are helpless before it, you cannot control it.

What do I do about you, Jay? What do I do when I can't do anything at all?

I see on Facebook that he will be on one of those news channels, talking about some complicated fiscal-slump thing that I have no idea about.

It is the first time I have seen him in months.

He is wearing a deep-blue tie.

He's fucking gorgeous.

I know he is nervous because the whole world has collapsed into the sum of the space he occupies, and his eyes are unsteady and he's trying to cover it up by nodding and making an expression of acute concentration.

He does this thing where he tips his head slightly when asked a question, as if accepting it. It is an accurate representation. Jay is the ultimate askee. When you ask him something, he takes it from you with a careful and sure hand, like it is important, like he's got it, no problem, no worries. Before answering, he thinks the query over, all of it. He looks at the sides and the underside, examines it up-close and from a critical distance. And because it's him doing this, because it is his stratospheric intellect being applied, whatever you asked him is elevated. Your questions grow in depth and dimension and texture. Because it is Jay Dhillon answering them.

And like so many other things about him, it sends me reeling. It swells my heart up with admiration-tinted affection, makes me afraid that my own body cannot hold all of me. It leaves me wishing, again, that I could just spill some of it in his direction, maybe into his arms.

Instead, I start looking for work.

———

Publishing-house events always threw DK into a foul mood. They had limited funds but for 'I don't understand *what* bloody reason' they also had one of the most distinguished guest databases amongst our clients, which meant that we had to put our best foot forward (and sometimes that included forgoing our cut with vendors) whether she wanted to or not. Book launches, evenings with authors, ICCR events with bad cheese and shitty wine—DK hated attending them all. I know this was because she considered spending an evening with the self-important socialites and the unprofitable celebrity of writers and elderly statesmen a colossal waste of her time. And I could see why, as the owner of an event-management agency, she would feel that way. But the truth was, I couldn't wait to attend one of those events myself, often spending hours at my desk imagining a run-in with Arundhati Roy and the inevitable fantastic conversation that would naturally follow.

'You're taking the Mansingh launch,' she told Ritika as her heels clicked out of the office and into the gleaming white Mercedes that she drove off in every day at five on the dot, somehow having completed more work than all of us put together in the four hours she had spent in the office.

I hadn't been at Fig Tree for very long, but just a couple of weeks had started to confirm what I should have suspected in the first place: a nine-to-five wasn't for me. I was lazy, and the pitiful salary that the job drew could hardly serve as any kind of motivation. I hadn't dragged myself out of bed before noon in years, scheduling only evening classes throughout the latter half of college, and the work itself was mindless—organizing small events, making calls to make sure we had enough Sula and chairs, and sending out endless email invites, personalizing each to make it look like it hadn't been sent by a twenty-two-year-old first-time employee bored out of her mind and counting down the minutes till she could leave the tiny cubicle that served as her office out in the backlands of the National Capital Region.

Fig Tree wasn't very large but it was quite successful, operating out of small, well-decorated offices in Noida. It was the first place that had called me back when I had sent out my resume, and my interview with DK had been enough reason to take the job.

'She's really—I mean, I've rarely met someone with such a zest for productivity, you know? It's inspiring!'

'Zest as in?' Ritika and Kiran, the two co-workers I was having lunch with, both looked confused.

'Mm, enthusiasm, but not exactly. More like eager to achieve goals and stuff.'

Kiran nodded. 'Oh, yes. No, she's very strict about our deadlines and events, okay? Don't mess them or she'll kill you.'

'No, no, that's not what I mean.' I chewed my zucchini stick thoughtfully, wanting to explain it properly. Both of them were really nice, and had been going out of their way to show me how things worked since my first bumbling day at the office. 'She's always going off about some new idea or event or something, you know, just—' I gestured with my hands, miming something blowing up.

'*Pataka!*'

'That's someone who is—'

I laughed, cutting off Kiran. 'A dynamo. Yes. Exactly. She's a total dynamo. And hey, I know what a pataka is, okay?'

Ritika laughed too as she gathered up the little steel bowls carrying her lunch of vegetables and rotis and yoghurt. 'No you don't, you firang.'

---

You'd never be able to tell from the brusque way she treated her (though to be fair, that was DK's general manner), but I strongly suspected that Ritika was her favourite employee. She was on a mission to teach us how to become the kind of strong, independent woman she herself seemed to be, and Ritika was her best student, a teacher's pet who escaped ridicule and resentment because of the sheer sincerity with which she operated. She was easily the hardest worker at Fig Tree and was saving up to pay for an MBA, all the while placating her orthodox Punjabi family and convincing them to let her have a job instead of a husband by waking up at four in the morning to cook and clean the house before changing two metros during her ninety-minute commute to work.

I admired her in the dubious way that people do when faced with someone who makes them feel grateful for the relative comforts of their own lives. Especially because despite what seemed to me like a harrowing schedule, she maintained both a sunny disposition and the kind of efficiency that made me wonder whether she actually lived in an alternate universe with about forty hours in the day.

She grinned and tsk'd when I posited this theory to her, gesturing to the well-worn blue notebook that was her constant companion.

'Everything gets done if you make lists and tick tick tick all through the day. You will start hating it when you miss a tick, and *bas*, all your work will get done.'

———

Her words came back to haunt me within a week, and I cursed myself for not taking her advice to heart.

SalT, an old favourite amongst Khan Market regulars, was reopening after being shut for a season (they said renovations, DK heard health violations). I had put off calling the numbers on the press list till the last minute, and as I woke to unexpected torrents of November rain on the morning of the opening, I knew I was screwed.

It was the first event that DK had entrusted me to oversee entirely on my own, and I was going to ruin it and disappoint her. I had to fix it somehow and there was pretty much only one way I could think of to do it. Panicking and on the verge of tears, I went and knocked on the side of Ritika's cubicle. She hesitated for a moment, much less than I thought she would, but as soon as I asked her what she thought DK would say when the owners of SalT called to complain that not one newspaper had carried a single mention of the reopening, she relented and started making calls. The long-standing media relationships that she had cultivated over her three years at

Fig Tree saved my hide, but it also meant that we had to switch our events for the day. It was risky manoeuvre, even though DK was out of town and unlikely to find out. I was suitably nervous as Ritika went to SalT to meet her contacts and do damage control, and sent me off to oversee her event.

It was a far grander affair than anything I could have handled, and as I walked through the familiar environs of the plush hotel (it housed the best sushi restaurant in town) and into the large room allocated for the book launch of a mildly famous, well-reviewed author, I found out why she had seemed so at ease letting me handle her event. Unlike all the haphazard little events I had been organizing as I wobbled about trying to find my feet, Ritika's launch party had been planned down to the tee, her careful attention to detail ensuring that anything I could think to look into had been checked and double-checked till everything was set to run smooth as jazz. I barely had anything to do, so I situated myself by one of the two sets of forty-foot doors at the entrance, smiling and ushering in guests as they arrived.

It was a pleasantly mindless occupation, and I started to relax as people trickled in. A few of them nodded an acknowledgement, though most didn't even seem to notice that there was a fellow human being saying hello to them as they swept themselves into the thickening crowd. I didn't entirely mind their rudeness because it let me space off into my own thoughts, but I was jerked out of them as I saw a familiar face and started to beam a greeting at it. I landed up smiling idiotically at the back of her dress as she brushed past the lowly employee standing at the door.

I'd met Mrs Lodhi many times, at many parties and weddings I had unwillingly attended with my parents. She had always been so nice, so interested in my life and full of questions about what I was studying in school.

A hot flash of anger licked at my throat as I thought about the fact that Ritika wouldn't think about this, that she would just consider this inherently disrespectful treatment as part of the job, and it was a struggle to keep myself looking pleasantly genial as I turned around to greet the next guest.

A small lifetime of what-if's, and just like that, reality had blended with the imagined.

Jay.

In a dark suit, blue tie in place, walking into the room, smiling a greeting, turning me instantly into a grenade.

I had to talk to him. I *had* to. His eyes had skimmed over me as he passed, but he hadn't recognized me. I hadn't expected him to.

I hadn't expected my feet to walk themselves over to him either, or for my right hand to gingerly tug at his coat sleeve.

'Hi.'

'Hi?'

I found my mouth glued shut by too much history, reduced back to six years ago because—no.

No. Let me just tell you what love is at seventeen.

At seventeen, he's a quarterback in the real world and you're still stuck in the linens of the schoolyard. He indulges you sometimes, tells you what lies ahead and shares a little of his life. Occasionally, he asks you something about yourself, and those moments when you are the centre of his attention become the highlights of your days and weeks and months and years.

At seventeen he is hopelessly, comically out of your league. Twenty-three and done with Princeton, saving the world with the beautiful girl he loves by his side, he is so far away that all you ever do is shake your head, laugh at yourself and head into second-period history.

But at seventeen, he's the boy who helped you when he didn't have to. At seventeen, he took the time to walk you to the decisions that would build your future. He told you to go ahead and be crazy, to take it all in and let it all out. He made you brave. And at seventeen you're bruise-free and don't know better than to be brave, to not be afraid to fall. So you fall, right into his words, starry-eyed and awestruck and most definitely in love.

'Mm, hi? Could I help you with something?'

The tousle of his hair, the pink pooling in the centre of his mouth, the line of his neck as he turned his head towards me—a straight, strong arrow from the lobes of his ears to the collar of his shirt.

'I—would you happen to have the time?'

And the justlovemeback is an impossibility, but that's okay, because you're seventeen and time is on your side. Time is on your side, Time has his arm slung around your shoulder and you're getting ice cream, you're friends. At seventeen, justlovemeback only hurts a little, only sometimes, because the world is wide open and no one has touched you yet. No one has loved you, no one has left you. No one has made you realize, yet, that you can never love someone enough to make them love you back.

Jay looked surprised. This must have been because he thought I had simply overlooked the fact that I was holding a cell phone bearing the time and not realized that I was, in fact, a gigantic, colossal moron who should never again be allowed to communicate with any other member of the human race, especially him. 'Of course. It's a quarter past eight.'

I mentally kicked myself and prepared to walk away. 'Thank you.'

It's hopeful. Even in its hopelessness, at seventeen, falling in love is the most hopeful thing in the world. Maybe because it happens so early on. Maybe because you spend the rest of your life trying to feel like that again.

But suddenly you're brushing twenty-three, and has it really been six years already? Six years watching in the shadows, six years waiting for him to notice you, six years of trying to shape yourself into something he could love without having any idea of what that is.

So you spend all this time growing up into whatever it is you were meant to be, and then one day, the universe comes alive at you, the frequencies create a sudden cacophony as they start to vibrate, and you think—why not? Six years and two days have passed. Everything else has moved on and still, and still, and still and always, you can want no one but him. It's time. Now or never, Tara, now or never. And sitting in your wrought-iron chair, on that patio, on a working Tuesday—like the first brownie, like the first drink and the first drag—you decide to take the plunge.

You fish around in your purse for a pen, and you put ink to a paper napkin. You could have tried to just say it, walked back up to him and let him remember you. But you wanted him to hold your words, to feel their weight in his hands and their strain on his mind.

You rationalize away the slight resentment (if I had given you less, if I had given you less than six years, would you even turn around?) and you're shaking; you can hardly hold the pen steady, you hope he won't mind the terrible handwriting.

Dear Jay,

I heartbreak-read the letter full of love you wrote to her. This is mine to you. To your swag, to your smile, to your white heart and black mind.

To the elegance of the bones on your right wrist, circled in the same red as mine.

I find now, the fifth time I rewrite this, that, yet again, all the words have staled. There are new things to love, again.

You can do anything. I've seen you ship ideas across the world, treat madness into art, flip through cultures like an ABCD textbook (that you could've written anyway), grow me up, feel me down and, even while removed a million miles in time and space, show me exactly what a man can do to a girl.

And it has been all these years where we have brushed past each other in single, solitary moments that have lain scattered like fairy dust upon my skin, which have all come together to make me know, without doubt or question, these few things—

I know you are the one for me. The only one who can keep up with (and race ahead of) me. The only one who will see the beauty in my insanity, who will take my hand and guide me around the dark instead of trying to pull me out of it. And love, I know I'm the only one who'll play piano for you on these keys, the only one who'll feel the whole story behind your scotch mouth, feel the gravity of your fingers, the weight of your mind along every line on my body.

I know that—for the soul only you can shake, for the life of breathless exhilaration only you can create, for all those things that are and that could be—it will always be you.

And I wait, in constant trepidation, for a terrible pronouncement—a new love, a death, an engagement, a marriage.

Love me. Let me love you. Give me the right to need you. You should know—I already do.

———

I told myself that I would wait to find the right time to give it to him and went back to man the door, automatically smiling and welcoming people in, asking them to please let me know if there was anything they needed. The party started winding down, white wine running dry, and autographed books, destined for decorative bookshelves, being carried out by manicured hands. My goodbyes met with even less acknowledgement than my hellos; alcohol had whittled pretensions at manners down to nought.

What had earlier just been a passing note in my mind now jangled my already edgy nerves. And when another person I recognized from another grand party swept by me as I greeted her, I heard my voice call out, 'Excuse me, ma'am, I was speaking to you.'

She turned around, her expression surprised. 'What?'

'I was just—I was greeting you. You . . .' I trailed off, the fight dying out of me as I realized what it could cost.

She stared at me for another moment in complete confusion, then turned around and walked away.

'Don't worry about it. Some day they'll all be scrambling over themselves to say hello.'

Jay, of course. Sharp rebuke on his face as he watched her go. A warm smile as he turned to me.

Kindness as a virtue is hard to fully appreciate until the dimming of youth. It grows in the lines that form, the creases near mouths, on foreheads and sprawling from the eyes. Not that I was entirely there yet, but I was beginning to see, beginning to understand that at some point, at some further bruised and weathered point, I would come to hold it dearer than anything else.

But right then, it hurt. It hurt me in some very visceral and necessary way, like the first flash of antibacterial on a fresh wound, and I couldn't stand still anymore. So I took myself outside, running by the time I got to the pool, shimmering deserted under cautionary lights. I took deep, desperate drags of a cigarette that did nothing. I'd have eaten the box whole if it would have helped.

I saw him come around the poolside to the leafy alcove I'd stopped at, following me calmly, as if girls crumpled and bolted from him all the time.

'That will kill you, you know.'

'I don't care.'

'You should.'

'I think I'm going to get fired.'

'Do you care?'

I exhaled, stubbing out the cigarette, almost laughing. 'No.'

He looked at me carefully, squinting, and I knew he was finding his way back to the water's edge, back by Caroline's fort.

'I know you.'

I nodded, letting myself cry now. It was safe. This was Jay.

He came over and hugged me, hesitant only for a moment, only for as long as he had to be.

'Hey, hey, what is it? Sweetheart, what is it?' His voice was still soft, warm wool, and it joined all the little spools of conversation I had stored away, but it was one too many, and I started overflowing. I had loved him too much for too long. It wasn't healthy. It had to come out.

'Tara.'

Soft, warm wool. Safety.

If this was the closest I was going to get to him, I had to make it count. I had to hand him the letter, shaking so hard I felt sick, and then start crying as he moved closer and held me, reading it somewhere above my shoulder.

We stayed there like that for a long time. I sobbed into the crook of his neck, clinging to him, and I can't remember now, because I was trying so hard not to get any salty tears on his suit, but I think he was holding me just as hard as I was holding him.

I had started to worry when the torrent of crying began to subside. As the hysteria that had made me throw sense and caution to the winds abated, the beginnings of alarm and panic began building.

But he had pulled us apart, gently, igniting a physical
memory so painful that I started sobbing again, thankful
to have something to do with my body, since spontaneous
combustion wasn't an option. And he had brushed my wet
hair off my hot face and kissed me on the forehead, then on
each cheek, then very, very softly, on the mouth. And he had
asked me just once whether I was going to look up, and when
I had shaken my head at the ground, held my hand and said,
'Okay, come on.' I had tried to fix my hair with one hand as
he led me through the lobby to the reception, and then into
an elevator, where I tried to reclaim my other hand to aid the
hair-fixing but was told in a very firm voice that said hand
would not be relinquished any time soon.

———

I couldn't remember when my body had just given out, turning
itself off for a while. But I woke up electric, like I hadn't slept
at all.

It had happened. It had all happened. I didn't for a moment
wonder whether I had imagined last night, or dreamt a very
real dream, because when you are that alive, when you are
a mass of sparking energy, when you are superhuman, a
humming lucidity is part of the package.

Still, I could hear my blood pounding as I picked up the
single white sheet on the pillow next to mine. It was thick and
expensive, embossed with the hotel logo—the kind of paper
that bore invitations.

*Dear Tara,*

*I know that as you go about your day, it is more than likely that you will play last night over in your mind a fair few times. And I know chances are that, after all your reconsiderations, you will settle upon regret, anger—at yourself and at me—and fear of what scary repercussions are to follow.*

I stopped reading. I put the letter down. My heart jumped into my lungs and I breathed three blank pages worth of shallow, panicked beats.

*But don't presume my feelings, dear girl, don't presume my thoughts and swim against the tide of human nature to place your faith in me. I do admit that it took me a moment to place you last night, but then, it has been some years and you are much changed. You must give me that, for I am not your run-of-the-mill idiot, you see. I consider myself rather special (☺) and so you should know some things as well—I am not unaware of how amazing you are, and I do have the sense to give you the consideration you deserve.*

*I have been in your place, so I know this is the hardest, craziest thing to do. You have shared something deeply personal and put yourself in a very vulnerable position. I absolutely respect that and wish more people had the guts to do it.*

*Six years. We have known each other for over half a decade now. And you are still so young—this must have lasted for much, if not all, of your adult life. Why did you never tell me, Tara? I wish you had told me.*

*Though perhaps I should have been less blind. I can, in retrospect, see a myriad clues spread out over the course of our few conversations over the years. I do not know why I consistently stuck my head in* the sand. Perhaps because you were still a child. Or maybe because the time was never right. Even now, time and circumstance play an interesting game with each other.

But you have ensnared my curiosity most singularly, and not only because last night can be considered a definite life-highlight. For in such few words, you have captured me more, and more of me, than most I have ever known.

I suspect that you might feel inclined to bolt for the hills upon reading this and disappear quite completely on me. But do not fray, dear girl. Do not run away. Let us see where life takes us.

Will you have dinner with me tonight?

# Dates

Dear Jay,

On the way to meet you, terrified and on the verge of turning the car around, I sent you a text saying the only thing I could think: I'm very nervous.

I regretted it right away. We are not close friends: we do not have the degree of relationship that allows for discarding the conventions of communication enough to speak of uncomfortable truths. But you replied: Surprisingly, I am as well.

Fire and rain, storm and shore.

I will hold that feeling of being pleasantly surprised very close to me. It happens but rarely, and starts to mean more and more as life jades you down by validating expectations of disappointment.

But this is how it always is with you. Always, I am excited and unsure, nervous and seventeen to the bone. But also always, I feel secure and cradled, settled-in with a knowledge that you've got it, nothing bad is going to happen as long as you're around—you won't let it.

249

I took a second at the entrance of the restaurant to try and compose myself, but ended up just staring at you. You. Waiting for me. For me.

I actually, physically felt myself become a cliché in that moment, wishing I'd had the sense to wear flats because, gosh, is this what going weak at the knees feels like?

It was a privilege to hear your thoughts and spend time with you. I love the way you talk, measured and steady, belying the brilliant chaotic madness of the ideas in your head. It is amazing how you are so many people wrapped into one, and I remember thinking there is little I want more in the world than to find out more about you. But at the time, I was having enough trouble sitting still in my seat and dealing with the pointy pain of blushing. Here's something men don't know: blushing hurts. Oh of course, it works as a natural rouge and can be quite becoming as a fluttering marker of femininity. But feeling like your cheeks are on fire feels like . . . your cheeks are on fire. It's very uncomfortable, blushing.

Between the dinner I couldn't touch and dessert, I grabbed the opportunity to get up and move around a bit by asking you to take a stroll by the koi pond outside the restaurant. I couldn't sit still anymore, I just couldn't. Not while my insides were roiling and dancing and generally being disobedient little children with no self-control. Later, when you paused to tell me why we were currently not making out, it occurred to me that you might have thought that's why I wanted to trace circles in the dark. It wasn't. I was just trying to breathe.

In the car on the way back home, I heard a Taylor Swift song play on the radio. I was about to turn it off reflexively, as is required of anyone wishing to preserve a shred of indie cred, but these words caught my ear—

It was enchanting to meet you

I had to stop and listen. And when I got home, I spent the rest of the night—well, doing a whole bunch of giddy, embarrassing things. ☺

Hope Greece goes well. I can hardly wait till next month.

Tara

---

Our second date was a substantial one. I received an envelope, embossed with Jay's last name and holding a ticket to Singapore. There was no note, no formal invitation or intimation. I was being asked to function on faith, and I loved it.

I called my mother, packed a bag and boarded the plane to Changi, feeling slightly guilty for missing work. It wasn't that I was a particularly fastidious employee and I knew Ritika would pick up my slack even if she didn't have to, but I spent the greater part of the flight resolving to be a better co-worker. However, then the pilot announced that we were about to land and nervous excitement took over.

I laughed out loud when I saw Jay waiting outside the airport, sweating through his suit and holding a bunch of wilting lilies.

'So, Mr Dhillon, what am I doing here?'

He grinned. 'Humouring my bad intentions.'

———

Jay had chosen well. Singapore was the best place to draw a week's worth of time out of forty-eight hours. It was alive all night and, away from home, we were completely free to take advantage of that.

We had a four-hour dinner at the Sentosa Quay, discovering a mutual love of fine chocolate and second-grade sushi. We found out that we both drank too much coffee and ate dosas and idlis when in need of comfort food, agreeing that our Punjabi and Bengali ancestors probably twitched in their graves every time we did so. He chastised me for smoking but bought me a pack when I asked, handing it over reluctantly.

'You're the only girl I've done this for.'

It wasn't a compliment. There was clear distaste in his voice. But there was also an admission, a singling out, an I-can't-believe-I'm-doing-this. I savoured the sentence with relish, holding it almost as close as a promise.

He drove us back downtown, past the pretty island and through the unapologetically urban roads of the city. I stared at his hand on the wheel, strong, sure, destined to hold mine. We moved closer to Fullerton Square, and through a vast, warm marble lobby into a cool, dark room. And then we were kissing and I was thinking that I had been waiting forever for this, so why the hell could I not stop concentrating on the fact that a whole day and night's worth of sharp stubble was razing my face? I tried to ignore it, but a particularly rough brush made me wince and Jay pulled away, concern clouding his voice. 'What's wrong?'

'Um, it's just, you know, sort of poking me? Just a little bit?'

He looked horrified, and opened his mouth, visibly struggling for a minute before saying, 'Oh, oh shit, I—wait—haven't you—I mean, are you—'

'No, NO! Oh! Not that! Your beard! Your face! Shaving … thing! Oh God! Not that!'

We burst out laughing at the same time, dissipating the tension into camaraderie. He excused himself to go shave, and when he came back out, he looked so young, like a little boy, like he must have looked at seventeen. It twisted my insides, and while precedent would indicate that I was in for a knee-buckling rush of nostalgic emotion, right then I only seemed capable of *not* thinking through a haze of desire.

'What?' He peered into the mirror over the dresser. 'Did I leave shaving cream on my face?'

I shook my head, some garbled half-words stuck in my throat.

He bent down, his face close to mine and—was I calling it right? Could he really be as nervous as I was?

'Hey, what?'

I swallowed. 'You look so nice.'

He broke into an abashed half-smile, and he looked down at his hands, introducing me to a shy dimple on his left cheek, flustered and so utterly adorable that I kissed him, quick, before my brain exploded with the effort of trying to compute the level of cuteness it was being exposed to.

He woke up with his hair in an almighty tousle, drooping into his eyes and sticking comically up in the back, looking even more of a kid than the night before. But he took his coffee all grown up—no milk, no sugar. Black. Hot.

We spent the morning in bed, talking. Towards afternoon, when our edges had been all but smoothed flat by discoveries and breakfast wine and skin on skin, I finally asked him about April.

'What was she like?'

'Do you really want to know?'

'Yes. I really do.'

'She was beautiful. Gorgeous. Brilliant. Bloody crazy, though.'

'You told me that, once.'

I saw a flash of anger cross his face. 'I shouldn't have done that.'

'I disagree. More, please.'

He smiled. 'She was very kind. She had a soft heart. Too soft, maybe. She was always breaking into pieces.'

I nodded, remembering. 'Did you end up putting her back together?'

'For a while, yes.'

'Do you miss her?'

'I do.' He sighed, tired. 'I miss who she used to be.'

'Who did she use to be?'

He sat up to look at me, piercingly, like he was trying to catch me in a lie. 'A lot like this, actually. A lot like you.'

Lying there with him, watching the flesh fall on to the bones of my dreams, I drifted into the blackest sleep of my life; safe, at last.

———

We woke up as the sun was glowing low in the sky, the golden light touching our skin with the kind of beauty all the make-up in the world couldn't achieve. We paid homage to it with our bodies, slowly, exquisitely. I rested on his chest, dwelling on the images, committing the plains of his face, the way light caught his angles, into the securest holds of my memory.

'This is my favourite time of day.'

'Because the day is dying?'

He kissed my nose. 'Because the night is just coming to life.'

We might have disappeared into each other again had my stomach not rumbled a firm protest. I hid under the covers, embarrassed, and he coaxed me out from under them, fondness warming his voice and my little fort of sheets. 'Let's go get you some dinner, love. It's almost nine. Come on, let's go before the night gets away from us.'

Time was following our lead, dancing with us, moments floating, flying, suspended. Gliding like water, flashing past like lightning. I had no handle on the hours, no control over how fast or slow they moved, and I couldn't have cared less. Because during those first heady months, we were at our best, we were unstoppable. He was the sweetest boy in the world when he had just shaved a decade off his face, and I the girl covering it with kisses, delighting in the simple magic of soap-scented skin. We were nice to everyone, our hearts glowing bright. We drove fast and drank slow, always just the perfect amount of alive.

———

Dear Tara,

When a man flies halfway around the world in curious anticipation, being able to cull only a couple of days thus to meet the object of his intrigue, he hardly expects to have his unrealistic expectations met.

I must confess I was rather surprised when you suggested we cap off our weekend by going to Level. You were so—what is the word— restrained, perhaps, during our first few dinners together that I would not have pegged you as the type for a loud, crazy club. But then, you seem to have made surprising-me-senseless something of a trademark, so I have happily resolved to just buckle in for the ride.

I have been reliving you in trails along my skin all through this flight. The elderly lady in 2B has been looking suspiciously over at me. I suppose the colour of my skin disbars me from exhibiting eccentricities without question.

Tara, I feel you coming for me. It is insidious, the way you have become incessant within my thoughts. I keep going back to our bodies aflame with dance upon the floor and the electric air between us on the ride back. The tumbling fall of hair all over your pretty face and the way you melted into me, shyness laced with need, my mouth slowly tangling you up with greed.

I feared my skin would be all but seared by the brush of your lips and tongue and breath, my eyes fixed forevermore upon the helpless lines of your body—the arch of your back, the stretched bones in your neck, and the fallen hollow in between them, where your heart beat so hard against me, ticking our seconds away.

You felt like something out of a movie, almost too good to be true.

It seemed I had lived an age in the anticipation of your skin sliding down me, and you, well, you locked between my legs. And when you pushed back your hair and looked straight up at me while—well, suffice it to say, dear girl, that was something else indeed.

# Dispersion

I only saw him in quick flashes, in between his trips to various corners of the world. He was a wizard troubleshooter, needed erratically and imperatively at various ports to sort out various issues. His work sounded fascinating: in the two months since we had been together, he had gone to Puerto Rico to quietly bribe a minister who was making trouble, then zipped off to China to woo another. And then to London to deal with a union and stopped off at Ukraine on his way back to Delhi, insisting that he couldn't tell me why, making me very nervous.

We managed to cobble together a few dates—the movies and dinners and busy public spots that are markers of togertherness—but whenever he was home we mostly spent what little time we had together in my apartment, avoiding his palatial home on Barakhamba Road. It could have been a warning sign, a marker of temporariness, but I never thought further into the future than four days ahead.

It turned into a sort of routine—a few days together, then weeks apart. Every time he left me behind, I wondered whether he was excited to leave, wondered whether he felt our time together like a stillness starting to settle upon him. I asked

him as much as I could about April, but I knew time had to
be given its due, and held off on more questions, held off on
asking for more of his time.

I had so much time to think and so much space to wonder
that fear began to tear at me. It was impossible not to see that
everything in the world could be a plaything of Jay's obscene
wealth—of money, of mind, of reach. Constant acquisition was
the only way to keep a spectacular boredom at bay. And once
the initial rush of fate and frequencies had stopped ringing in
his ears, how long would it take for Jay to move on from me?

———

this chair is blue
and this bed is bare
and this floor is cold—
to my touch

this is a small table
and this door creaks
and this sink holds capillaries—
the breath and the blood

these walls are green
and this paint is peeling
and this is a can of coke—
spread upon the floor

this air is thin
and this hand is not moving
and this life is fading

into nothing. We're going to become nothing. Nothing-is-something, big deal. Hamlet could hold up my skull, make divine clichés in my name, and I won't even fucking know. That's what scares me most of all. The not knowing. Of what lies beyond, yes, but also the little things. I'm dead, but did Thomas marry David? What was the movie of the year, the year after I left? What are the songs I'm missing out on? What fashion is recycling its way to ramps? I see they're shutting down that shady restaurant with the rubbish Chinese; what's coming up in its place? Hopefully a decent coffee shop. But let's be honest, they're probably going to stick another damn tikka takeaway there. Cubes and cubes of dead meat just staring out the window.

———

Dearest Jay,

It's debilitating, this wretch of being away from you, this transformation of my days into sand slipping through a faulty hourglass, every grain escaping faster than the last.

As much as I long to hear your voice over the cracking lines of a call from Saigon, telling me about your day in the way that tells me I am your person, I ache to feel the textures that slide over me in layers—the fine wool of your suit giving way to the crisp linen of your shirt, buttons an eternal hindrance—the only barrier between my skin and yours. I love your skin, Jay. I love it and I love you. I love you.

When will you come home?

———

When I called him, I heard the sounds of an important meeting—the shuffles of suits in a boardroom, signatures rustling paper and the clink of bad coffee. Can you come over, Jay? Can you come to me? It's important, yes. You know I wouldn't ask if it wasn't.

When his shoes clicked into the apartment, I was already slipping out of consciousness and deeper into the tub, my stomach burning as the pills melted inside me.

He was so angry. I wasn't sure how long it had been between that afternoon and waking up in my own bed with him sitting beside me, though the deep shadow of beard across his face told me it had been a couple of days. As the world sharpened into focus, I registered how angry he was, the lines on his forehead, the tightness of his grasp and mouth.

He had hurt. He cared. I felt relief wash over me like mental morphine, dragging me back to sleep.

I woke up again as the sunlight was ebbing away, went out and found him sitting at the dining table, nursing a glass of scotch, the bottle next to it almost empty.

Even after all these years (and yes, you can argue that twenty-three years is not that many, but the perception of time is the most goddamn relative thing in the world) I knew nothing of my mind. I could never predict its movements, the arcs it would follow and where it would land me up. I had yet to know my own mind, yes, but I did know my body. I knew it intimately. I knew it to be stubborn when it came to getting warm, resilient when I asked it to pull through forty hours before a deadline, and quiet, too quiet, when left to itself.

So I called to mind the first time we kissed, the bridge that unfurled ahead of and behind us, the sound of baying wolves, the lights dusting a Piccadilly sky. The memories set me ablaze, as always. They reddened my cheeks and brightened my eyes, tightened up my body and brought out the bones that lay at the base of my neck. This was instant make-up, and I made myself up with the memory that moved me most, for the person I loved the most.

'Jay.'

'How could you do that?'

'Won't you come to me?'

When we kissed, I felt so much of myself drain into him that for a while it was just my empty body, soulless and weightless, pressed to his mouth, clung to his chest. Have you ever felt like that? Like the person you're holding is all that's holding you together?

His lips worried around mine, and he pulled away.

I kissed him again. He pulled away again, looking scared, like he knew.

'Do you know that when you walk into a room I can feel all the great dreams and desires of my life collapsing into the sum of the space you occupy?'

And his eyes clouded over, like they should, like they had to.

It's the headiest rush in the world, this look. It says, quite simply—I want you. There are a million other things to be thinking about right now, a billion other people out there, but I can't even acknowledge anything else for wanting you so badly, dear girl.

Jay's hands were cushioning my head against the wall. They would bruise, and I revelled in knowing that he didn't care. The concern in his lips had been replaced by an irreverent need and we kissed deep, teeth and tongues greedy to taste, to feast. The momentary breaks to breathe were unbearable, so his fingers tightened fistfuls in my hair and I put my face into his neck and smelled him underneath soap and cologne and his mouth bruised a line along my collarbone and I folded a leg up and around him and we couldn't have made it to the bedroom. Hell, we didn't even make it to the floor.

*March 2014*

# Letters

There were two letters in the mail, postmarked from Berne.

*Dear Love,*

I was so happy to get your letter. It has been quite unpleasant here recently. Germany's cold is the kind you feel down to your nerves. Even when you are warm inside, you cannot help but be aware that it is out there, that horrible winter.

I have been missing you greatly. I have missed having your words arrive in the mail, missed seeing the ink collecting in blotches as you collect yourself. So it gave me much joy to see that you have written, especially given that I left you after that unpleasant incident.

I was so happy, but—I don't know. Not quite happy entirely, do you know? I sometimes think I don't know how to be happy at all. At other times I think it has to do with you, that some of your sadness has seeped so deep into me that now I cannot escape it.

Lately, I have been dreaming rather strange dreams.

Perhaps the strangest thing about them is that I do not always have to be asleep for them to begin.

There is one that has become a most frequent night-time visitor.

In this dream, you are dying. Slowly, bit by part. Cancer, of course. When they had to take your poisoned breasts, you cried and cried and said you didn't want me to touch you because you didn't feel like a girl anymore. I kissed you anyway, obviously. How could I not?

I kept remembering lying face-down in your hair.

My left hand on your right breast (now a memory and sometimes a phantom handful), my body spilling over yours, my face in your hair. Upturned in your hair. Nose-down in your hair. Smelling your hair. White jasmine and your sex-sweat. Your sex-sweat smells different from your normal sweat. You smell different when I hug you after your return from your manic runs from when I lie face-down in your hair, happily immobile.

As the chemicals kept going in, your hair started falling out.

And I realized I must learn to love a you minus all these things I loved about you. I must, I must learn.

I dream of this before I sleep and it is one of the good dreams, dramatic and poignant. I play it often, savour it slowly, sometimes till the end and sometimes only a little bit.

And I keep thinking how you too—the Tara of my reality, the Tara of flesh and bone, the Tara who will not eat carbs after dark and looks at me like she's trying to drink me in—will slowly burn out. You will age, my dear, you will go old and grey. And I grieve for the beauty you will lose, for the shadow of what you are now that you will become. I grieve for the places my hands and lips like to run down. The watered silk of your back that will turn to weathered parchment. The symphonic curves of your body that will wither and shrivel into a memory of loveliness. A memory of you at your finest. You will become a memory even as you live and breathe, my love, and I can hardly bear the sadness of that. I can hardly bear it at all.

But I digress, don't I? Returning to the subject of my confession, I find that, differing only in the details, all my dreams are like this. There is always some sort of tragic ending. I cannot seem to conceive of a happy one.

Things seem like they are at a standstill. My life feels stagnant. I seem to be frozen and unsure of where to go.

I do not know but, as I said, I sometimes think I don't know how to be happy at all.

All my love to you, dear girl.

Jay

———

Tara,

I have been sitting here for several hours, determined to remember.

The first time I saw you, you had seemed so lost, standing alone, forlorn. Looking out over the sun dying upon the water.

The memory has sharpened.

I remember taking a chance and postulating one of my stranger thoughts. It was possible—truly, it was expected—that you would not catch on; I was ready to steer my words to ordinary ground.

But you had understood. I remember that. You had understood me.

I recall, during our sporadic communications, being surprised by how much of yourself you revealed to me. I would have been flattered had I not recognized you instantly—I knew so well what it felt like to be you. To walk around like an exposed nerve, to not to know how to draw up the covers necessary for survival. I saw that you, child that you were, knew loneliness like few ever will and I felt so sorry for you.

Do you remember what I had told you about us, once, long ago?

It was something I had said in passing, during a conversation that I have only now, after so many hours spent staring at the sun sliding off walls, retrieved from some intractable fissure hidden deep within the recesses of my consciousness. 'We are not happy unless we are crying'—that is what I had told you. Do you remember?

I am going to Berlin tomorrow and must chain myself down there for a week.

Will you come to me, dear girl? Will you forgive me and come?

# Crack the Spine

The next day, I forced myself to wake up earlier than usual so I would be the first one in the office, and asked DK for an indefinite amount of time off. I phrased it as a request and not the resignation that it really was.

'Why?'

'I have to leave the country for a while.'

'I see. And where are you going?'

'Um, Germany. A friend needs me.'

She looked at me for a moment, then burst out laughing. She sat down, took her glasses off and rubbed the corner of an eye. Shaking her head, she put her glasses back on and, amusement still glowing on her face, said, 'Man, you rich kids are really consistent, I have to give you that. Go, go. Just be careful. You're a sweet girl, but I've seen a hundred of you walk in and out of my doors, and all of you think you're so silly, so crazy, so beautifully broken and that this—your lack of purpose and discipline—you all think it's some vitally important thing. You want these jobs to serve as playthings and distractions, and I have to, I mean, I'm forced to give them to you because on paper—' She stopped, all traces of amusement replaced by anger. 'You all think it's something beyond the fact that you have never known a true worry. Have you? Have you ever known a true worry?'

I shook my head, because what else was I supposed to do?

DK continued to stare me down, but her sharp eyes were more than just angry. To this date, I can't be certain, but every time I think back upon the scene, I seem to remember a shade of pity tinting them. Finally, she sighed and looked back down at her iPad, reaching for her glasses.

'You'll get half this month's pay. Go. Be careful. Try not to entertain yourself into an early grave.'

———

By the time I touched down in Berlin, the windowpanes had already turned that lavender of first light, calming me, reminding me that morning breaks the same everywhere.

Jay met me at the airport and we stepped straight into a winter storm. Sharp icicles of wind pierced our cheeks, making them feel soft, making us 'feel alive, Tara. Isn't it really something—the way the deadness of a snowy winter makes your blood rush around so?'

As we waited for a taxi, I started to lean against his parchment frame for warmth, ignoring the warning signs because I didn't have the energy to confront them.

Our turn came. Heated leather warmed us through our cold clothes as we slid away, and I moved closer to Jay, snuggling up to him, begging his body to thaw the parts of me the hot air inside the taxi couldn't reach. He bent his head down and we kissed, we kissed deep. In the periphery of my consciousness, I heard the taxi driver laugh a cruel little laugh.

It irritated me, pricked me through winter-blushed skin. 'What's so funny?'

Jay gave me a look. Shut up, Jay, let me be rude. Everyone is allowed to crack sometimes.

'You two in love, yeah?'

'Absolutely.' Why was Jay so calm? Why was all the defiance here mine? 'How far to the hotel, sir?'

'Why were you laughing?' Why was he laughing? What was funny here?

His accent was thick but the grammar was perfect. 'Don't you know that the new girl is always better?' He turned around, pale green eyes on black skin, teeth baring white into me, square winter icicles splicing me wide open.

'Pull over.'

'Tara, we're in the middle of the highway. He can't—'

'Jay, just make him pull the fuck over'

'Tara, calm down—'

'Jay—'

I had to have been screaming, but I wouldn't know till later, when I came to, in a soft, white, warm winter hotel bed.

———

'What the hell happened in there?'

'I'm worried about you.'

'It's making you sick.'

'I need you to be okay, Jay.'

We spent the days inside the hotel room, under the covers. Jay talked in his sleep, fractured sentences that never found their way to a period.

'Dear girl, dear girl, are the great sweeps of beauty worth it, dear girl? I can't quite seem to calculate it right. Maybe I lied to you, dearest child, why say it if I—'

A soft, warm spool of wool coming undone, melting into his madness with an acquiescence that told me there was no saving him.

'The new girl. April was the new girl. And then she just wasn't, anymore, at all. And you, Tara? You?'

I would never really have him, would I? No. Jay belonged only to himself. In his blue world, he was unreachable. I had been pushing away the incoming clarity, but here it was—the acute loss of his endless heart, broken into a shape only I could find beautiful.

'I am afraid, oh dear girl, I have become afraid—'

I had spent my whole adult life leading up to Jay, and now, for the first time, I felt it a terrible burden. Up-close, he was exhausting. It was just so exhausting, this hardbound agony of being in love with an irreparable man.

Had I known it would come to this? Perhaps. The faults along his mind had always been visible to me. But how could I not love them, how could I not love him? They were mirrors of mine, after all. And underneath it all, wasn't he still the boy who had held my hand by the water and moved me to music only we could hear?

———

'I want to give you something.'

Jay looked down at me nestled in the warm space between his shoulder and jawline, flashing a teenage grin. 'I mean, if you insist . . .'

I laughed, realizing only then that I hadn't done so in what felt like a very long time. 'Such a pervyperv.'

He brushed his lips against my ear and whispered, 'Oh, you're going to pretend to be a good girl now, is it?'

'Only for a minute. I really have to do this, Jay.'

He disentangled us and sat up against the headboard. 'All right, all right. What is this terribly important thing that must delay me from having you?'

'There's this song. This beautiful, incredible song that not enough people have heard. I want you to know it. I need to know that you know that part of me.'

He pulled it up on his phone and, as he discovered it, I repeated the derived prayer inside myself like a litany.

*We are the living. So relate us, to brand new words on yellowed pages, to ancient words from sharp-tongued sages. Form our words, form our phrases. It's true; all we are, all the volumes, all the wisdom, are all just words we knew before. Blame is placed, punctuate it. And we'll read the lines, we'll mark the ages.*

'Great lyrics.'

'The words are—' I paused, looking for words. 'The first line. Crack the spine. I—do you ever feel like that, Jay? Do you ever feel brittle, like you're being opened up, like your skin is splintering at the spine?'

He looked at me, hard. Almost angry, a little scared.

'Yes.'

'What's wrong?'

'What do you mean?'

'You sound angry.'

'Do I?' He sighed and closed his eyes. 'Of course I do. Brittle. Of course. All the time.'

I nodded, satisfied. I knew he'd get it.

I always try to bear this. Every day is a struggle against this tremendous sense of loss. Every hour, every minute, everything lost is lost. It truly is lost. And as time passes, I count the minutes down, I lose the people and as I lose the people, I lose the places. 'We start with a whole world to own, and then we lose it all, piece by painful piece.'

Say something, Jay. Help me.

'What's that people like to say? "Time heals everything."'

I bit into his words with grateful venom. 'That's bullshit. Time just erases everything.'

He nodded. 'Life is nothing but a series of relentless chasms left behind by people who have been loved.'

Prickled, pickled grief, so quick to turn to hostility.

I turned, hostile, 'Why would you say that? How does that help me?'

But he was angrier than I was, his voice softer, his words harder.

'Do you know what you did, Tara? When you wrote me that letter, do you know what you did? Do you?'

'What—'

'And I let it go along. Of course I did. How could I not?' He stopped, and his sharp anger thawed into a spreading sadness. He closed his eyes and lay back, breaking his voice and my heart in one fell breath. 'How could I have not, Tara? You were beautiful, and that was the least interesting thing about you.'

'What're you saying, Jay?'

'You can't do without pain, can you?' He asked it slowly, so slowly that we both knew it wasn't really even a question.

'I want to be happy, Tara. I just want to be happy. White-picket-fence-with-a-big-fucking-dog happy.'

'Do you?'

'Dear girl, can you?'

He wasn't asking and I didn't want to know. My heart was pounding out of my chest, it was in my throat, it was blocking my voice so that everything sounded muffled and unclear when I said, 'Who's going to make you happier than me, Jay? Who's going to try harder?'

He shook his head. 'That's the problem, my dear girl, isn't it? They're not the same thing.' He moved closer to me, held my wet face up to his. 'You'll try so hard, you'll break yourself.'

My face was in his hands and I knew the answer, but I asked him anyway. 'Won't you save me?'

—————

I woke up with a start.

Frequencies.

—————

It wasn't just that he was standing what would be considered, by any reasonable measure of safety, dangerously close to the edge of the bridge. It was more the airlessness in his stance, his feet merely skimming the ground, like he could take flight at any moment.

The fall would be beautiful, a graceful arc ending in a brilliant spark as his body broke the still, dark water. Jay had a flair for the poetic that everything he did seemed bent in obedience to. Even the night sky was compliant to him, shrouding the moon in clouds, diffusing its tacky white light into a feathery glow.

If I let him, Jay would die. It would be the same world—but without Jay in it.

And I knew it would have been a certain sort of kindness to just let him go. If we are ever part of a greater struggle than fighting to stay alive, it is fighting to want to stay alive. But overcome by a loathsome, helpless selfishness, I could not be kind.

'Please, won't you stay?'

'It would be such a relief, dear girl.'

My mind's eye raced ahead of reality, and there I was, in a world that was the world, but without Jay in it. It really wasn't anything at all, was it? Just a place, roads and ground, with people and shops and cats and things. And I thought perhaps it wasn't what Jay was, but what he meant to me. Without him anchoring me into meaning, into reality, my own life seemed inconceivable.

'Please don't go, Jay.'

It had been a colossal favour to ask.

'How did you know I was here?'

'I just knew.'

'How, though?'

A bright fire was lighting up the water, and like Caroline, just like that poor fool, I knew the ship was sinking.

'I think there's a layer, somewhere in the atmosphere, where the frequencies of our feelings are stored.'

'Tara—'

'Jay, I know why Caroline ran to the ship.'

'Caroline?'

'Caroline. Don't you remember? From the first time we met? At that wedding by the old fort.'

'Oh, yes. Of course, of course.'

'I know why she ran to the ship.'

Jay smiled at me, through my tears and his. 'Why did she run to the ship?'

I started laughing. 'She was trying to save him.'

He held out his hand and I tucked it into place, wound his fingers with mine. We stood side by side, at the blurry edge of the bridge, looking out over the dark water for a very long time.

———

Jay ended things with me before he left Berlin.

Our hearts were too alike, our hurts too much the same. I know he thinks he made a wise choice and I wonder whether he always will. For a week, we had stood helplessly by and watched my sadness seeping into him and his into me. We had marinated in each other's madness, tasting the chips of pain like burnt cinnamon upon our tongues.

My dreams hadn't taken reality into account and, as I watched us slowly crumble into each other, I was so very sorry to have pulled us together.

'We were the only ones who could hear the music, Jay.'

'You can't light a match in a room filled with fireworks, Tara. Not even if you're careful. No matter how hard you try.'

For another seven days, I wandered around the city reconciling myself to the fact that unlike the other places I had prowled when wounded, Berlin would forever be a stranger to me. I felt no kinship with its people, no desire to excavate meaning from their language. I saw no humour in the silly bears, no beauty in its strong buildings and wide streets. When it was time to leave, I got into a taxi headed for the airport and made the decision to reach for it. It was so easy, and it was lying right there: white picket fence and a big fucking dog. A life with an Instagram filter sitting pretty on top of it—Valencia or Rise, one of the brightshinyhappy ones.

Daylight was melting into the Kurfürstendamm as I took my place on the horizon, on the edge of walking into a sunset that would be mine alone. And I felt a great hope rise within me. I think it is going to be okay. I think we might have escaped.

*December 2015*

# Epilogue

Deep yellow sun, dusty yellow sky. Anaya Arora after school.
  Light brown hair loosed from a braid, like wisps of satin,
like bits of silk.
  Seventeen,
  So easy on the eye.

————

It was a blue January morning. Cold, but not clear. The sky
dropped glaring hints of rain. Vir Dhillon looked up at the
clouds outside his bedroom window, then down at the lawns
below, where a hundred little penguin-suited figures were
scurrying around setting up tables decked in white linen and
Baccarat crystal. Sighing, he sent up a silent prayer for the rain
to hold off for at least a few hours.
  He turned back to the mirror, inspecting himself in all his
wedding regalia. Almost, he thought, I'm almost good-looking.
He didn't like the sharp downturn of his nose, or the way his
hair refused to sit still, but he went to the gym thrice a week

and had himself sewn into Ford and Zegna and he made the effort and he was almost good-looking.

Reminding himself to check his persistent instinct for self-reflection and concentrate on checking the fit and fall of his midnight-black Rathore silk, he swept his eyes along the length of his frame, looking for faulty details. There were none, of course.

He quirked a quick smile. These were his moments, the small victories he scored for himself and himself alone. How can you wear black to a wedding, beta? How can you wear black to your *own* wedding?

The smile slipped off his face as he felt a momentary current of memory break through the surface of his consciousness like a drowning man flailing up for one last, desperate breath.

It had to have been, what, four years ago? Five? That one-line email in his inbox: `I liked the black`. He remembered it had piqued his curiosity. He had meant to reply to it when he had a spare moment, but then an important call had come in from Saigon, and there had been problems with the crackling line, and, once deciphered, more problems relayed, and it wouldn't do; they couldn't contain the situation, he would have to get over there right away.

He wondered when the image of Anaya's naked body would replace the one that persisted in dogging him, wondered it only in the periphery of his consciousness, letting it happen without acknowledging it into existence. But Jay decided he should—he would—drink to her. Not from his usual decanter of Walker Blue, but a slow, mellow cup of Daiginjo. As he drank, he made a concentrated effort to stay on the bridge; to dive in now would be to drown. And when the sake started taking full effect, he determinedly sidestepped the memory of the shadow that had flickered across Anaya's face and settled in her eyes after his fifth glass of clear gold liquid at the sangeet.

It passed so quickly that he didn't really even have time to register it. Like a little lick of lightning, he felt a sudden jolt of thick, unadulterated, punch-to-the-gut sadness. It was a disconnected sort of sadness, though. Vir didn't feel entirely in possession of it, sensed he was holding on to it for someone else. And yet, he felt very full, very filled, like he had eaten it out of another person, leaving behind an empty body, weightless and free.

His fingers itched to write about the sensation before the lingering after-effects evaporated, taking with them the spark of inspiration that he felt far too rarely these days. It had been so long since he had cracked open a spine, so long since he had stained his hands inky blue with a cheap old fountain pen and come out, on the other side of forty-two caffeinated hours, with thousands of words. Words full of him, full of the madness that made him want to weep for joy, for the relief of having released them and for how much like himself he had felt.

But that would have to wait, wouldn't it? Vir was marrying Anaya. No, Virvardhan Dhillon was wedding Anaya Arora. It was done. The future had been signed. The future did not hold cracked leather spines weathered from constant dives into the pages. The future did hold, however, the distinct possibility of stratospheric success and contentment passable as happiness. That was something. That was definitely something.

Life on cue, there was a knock on the door. That would be the round, pink face of Dorchester, cobbled with early folds and split into a grin from ear to ear. He would have been sent up by an array of aunts and cousins who had painted themselves permanent fixtures in Vir's life for the occasion. I can't believe you're actually getting married, bhaiya! Sit here, beta, sit next to Panditji—do you know what you're supposed to do?

Dorchester, though, had actually been around for some time now, ever since Barakhamba Road met Mayfair during freshman orientation at Princeton and discovered a mutual love of Calculus, Apple Jacks and leggy redheads. Now, Vir returned his grin, both of them back, for an instant, on the way to crew at the lake, rising American sun fresh in their eyes.

In the recesses of his consciousness, Vir noted that Dorchester had never said a thing to him about his fiancée. He questioned, briefly, the fact that his closest friend hadn't made the jokes required to sign off the last few days of bachelorhood, made none of the bawdy mentions men are expected to make about the marital bed. But that was the thing about Anaya. You didn't discuss her porcelain restraint. You didn't crack a dirty quip about her measured manners. She was perfect. Quite perfect. Bulletproof, really.

'Ready?'

An ancient priest tied the ancient knot. He pulled it tight, because some sixth sense sharpened by ninety-three wizened years told him to provide extra insurance to the union being formed. She placed her henna-adorned, gold-encrusted hands in Vir's, and his fingers reflexed into the merest suggestion of a protective caress. Her bangles clinked together in his wet palm, the sound muffled by the pitter-patter of the first few winking drops of rain.

The moment was here. It was about to happen. Everything was waiting.

As the timeless, ageless chanting began gluing their dynasties together, he looked at her for a long minute. First, at her face, which was lowered and lit by the flickering fire—she was shy and beautiful and alive in the way that only a bride can be.  And then, as he looked at her hands, encased in his, pouring samagri into the flames, he found himself unable to stop imagining those same hands, wrinkled and lined thick with veins, pouring the grey dust of his ashes into the Ganges, letting the blue water swallow him whole.

# Thanks, guys.

Okay, full disclosure: I'm lazy. I'm as stay-in-bed-all-day, let-the-dishes-pile-up, buy-new-clothes-instead-of-doing-laundry lazy as they come. So the fact that this book actually exists right now is a miracle and a testament to what the unflagging support of an incredible network of people can do.

Thank you so much to my parents—I will (literally and figuratively) never be able to pay you back.

Thanks as well to Gandharv Roy, Payel Chatterjee and Prateek Mookerjee—they didn't do much, but they know where I live.

Apologies to my wonderful editors, Nimmy and Purnima, for my frequent misinterpretation of the word 'deadline', and thanks for taking a chance on me.

Thank you to Aditya Berlia for all the help, John Paul Roney for letting me use his words, and the beautiful, glorious Achala Upendran for actually making this happen.

And thank you to Bum, for reading and rereading endless bad drafts, and never letting me forget that, at the heart of it all, there lay a story worth telling.